Praise for Becky Barker's *Cade's Challenge*

"Cade's Challenge" is the epitome of the steamy romance novel. The chemistry between Cade and Sallie was combustible and their love scenes so hot, I swear I saw steam rise from the pages. The mystery is interesting and unpredictable, but the real story is the romance, and I enjoyed watching it unfold. It's an intriguing, romantic, and ultra sexy story, and I highly recommend it."

~ *Debbie, Once Upon a Time Reviews*

5 Lips "Cade's Challenge is an exciting and sensual tale by talented Becky Barker. Cade is an Alpha man to adore... for me, the emotions of the love scenes make the book the awesome read it is. Cade and Sallie share a passion that is intense and erotic... a wonderful story I highly recommend."

~ *Tara Renee, Two lips Reviews*

"*Cade's Challenge* is an incredible read... The sexual tension is so fiery my monitor was smoking... With so many twists and turns, I was kept guessing the identity of the stalker until the ending. Becky Barker did a marvelous job with this story. Of course, I don't believe I have ever read a bad story by this wonderful author."

~ *Shayla, Romance Junkies Reviews*

"Cade obviously had feelings for Sallie that were passionate, and the suspense of who was stalking them was intense. I was thrilled to learn that Becky Barker had written a story for Cade. I had absolutely adored him in On Wings Of Love."

~ *Kathy Andrico and gottawritenetwork.com*

Cade's Challenge

Becky Barker

A Samhain Publishing, Ltd. publication.

Samhain Publishing, Ltd.
577 Mulberry Street, Suite 1520
Macon, GA 31201
www.samhainpublishing.com

Cade's Challenge
Copyright © 2008 by Becky Barker
Print ISBN: 1-59998-740-6
Digital ISBN: 1-59998-477-6

Editing by Laurie Rauch
Cover by Vanessa Hawthorne

This book is a work of fiction. The names, characters, places, and incidents are products of the writer's imagination or have been used fictitiously and are not to be construed as real. Any resemblance to persons, living or dead, actual events, locale or organizations is entirely coincidental.

All Rights Are Reserved. No part of this book may be used or reproduced in any manner whatsoever without written permission, except in the case of brief quotations embodied in critical articles and reviews.

First Samhain Publishing, Ltd. electronic publication: May 2007
First Samhain Publishing, Ltd. print publication: March 2008

Dedication

This story is dedicated to four very special people who've brought infinite joy to my life—Konor, Emily, Jadyn and Allison. I love each of you for your unique personalities, your endless fascination with the world, and your sweet baby innocence.

With many thanks to my loyal readers who waited so long for Cade and Sallie's story. I deeply appreciate your continued support and enthusiasm.

Chapter One

Hidden in the late-night shadows, he watched as the lights went off in the house. Watching, always watching. He waited a while longer, and then he made his move.

ಬ೩෮

Sallie Archer hovered on the edge of sleep, its tantalizing promise edging closer with each tick of the clock. The familiar comfort of her big bed, combined with mental and physical exhaustion, brought another hectic day to a close. Her muscles went limp and her brain slowly relinquished all thoughts and worries.

Suddenly, an unfamiliar sound jarred her awake again, jerking her back to consciousness. Fighting the pull of fatigue, she lifted heavy eyelids and let her eyes adjust to the darkness of the room.

Movement to the right of her bed startled her and made her go numb with shock. She watched in horror as a man slipped through her French doors, leaving them ajar as he crept past the foot of her bed toward the opposite side of the room. He glanced her way, and she stopped breathing.

Sallie's chest constricted. He muttered something, his tone low and suggestive, then told her he'd be right back. All her breath got trapped in her lungs and they started to burn. Her stomach alternately clenched and roiled as panic washed over her. Her heart pounded brutally. She watched, frozen with terror, as the sinister figure finally stopped staring her way and disappeared into the living room.

A rush of blood clamored in her ears, deafening her when she most needed to hear. She had to move, to do something before he returned, yet she wasted precious time frozen with fear. *I won't be immobilized by fear! I won't be immobilized by fear!* She chanted the childhood refrain, but she still couldn't move a muscle.

Calm down. Calm down, she mentally commanded herself and dragged in a soundless breath. Maybe she'd imagined the ghostly image. Living alone sometimes made her feel vulnerable, especially at night, when dreams tended to tangle with reality. She strained to hear sounds from the living room and heard the quiet thud of footfalls on the carpet.

This was no dream.

She needed to call 9-1-1 and get help. With what seemed like superhuman effort, she mustered the strength to lift her arm toward the nightstand and her portable phone.

Damn! It wasn't there. Swallowing a sob, she remembered carrying it to the bathroom earlier. Her habit of leaving it all over the house was an irritation, but she'd never imagined it might get her killed.

Her next thought was escape. Fear had her momentarily paralyzed, while the instinct to flee warred with the instinct to lie still and not draw attention to herself.

She could get out the same way the intruder had gotten in, and pray he didn't see her. The security light shone brightly through the sheer lace curtains of the French doors. It beckoned her, suggesting safety.

Before she could make a run for it, she had to unlock limbs that were frozen in fear. Another silent sob clawed at her throat as she forced her reluctant muscles to cooperate. With slow, cautious movements, she eased from the bed. Listening intently, she waited until her trembling legs would support her. She wanted to be able to run once she'd cleared the terrace.

Taking a deep breath, she bolstered her courage and slipped across the room, and then quickly darted through the doors. The warm spring air assaulted her senses as she left the cool of the air-conditioned room. The sudden change in temperature caused goose bumps on her goose bumps. Her feet tingled as rough concrete replaced plush carpeting, the feeling racing up her quivering legs.

In the next instant, she turned and slammed into a very tall, broad-shouldered man. They collided with a thud and she sucked in her breath, her heart pounding frantically in her chest. Her muscles constricted as renewed panic surged through her, and all she could think to do was fight.

Fists balled, she started swinging wildly, pummeling his chest and shoulders until he grasped both her arms and locked them against her sides. He mumbled something, but she was too panicked to hear. It had been years since she'd felt so helpless and afraid, but she'd vowed never to be victimized by another man. With her arms trapped, she started kicking, refusing to succumb to his overpowering strength.

He pressed her against the building, the weight of him firmly anchoring her in place. He was hard and heavy, nearly suffocating her as he tried to still her frenzied thrashing. Her lungs burned, and she struggled for air as his head dipped closer.

"Shh, Sallie, it's Cade," he whispered near her ear. "Stop fighting me."

The sound of her name stalled her rising hysteria. She froze, trying to absorb what she'd heard while struggling to drag air in and out of her tortured lungs. With supreme effort, she stopped thrashing and forced herself to concentrate.

Even though she was pinned to the wall, this intruder wasn't forcing himself on her. He'd only tried to stop her from lashing out at him. The voice, though a muffled whisper, held the familiar cadence of Cade Langden's low, sexy drawl.

Once her breathing had calmed a little more, her mind started to clear, too. Her senses began to register the scent and feel of the man whose body pressed fully against hers—chest-to-chest, stomach-to- stomach, thighs-to-thighs.

A whiff of familiar aftershave drained more tension from her. The blinding haze of fear slowly cleared from her vision. His distinct features came into focus; the ruggedly handsome face with strong jaws, a straight nose, sensuous mouth and firm, stubborn chin. Caramel-colored eyes framed by thick, dark lashes stared into hers. They were the deep, warm eyes of a man she'd trust with her life.

Her body went slack with relief. She would have crumbled, but he gathered her close. Sallie exhaled a ragged sigh and slipped her arms around his waist, dropping her head to his shoulder. The pounding of his pulse echoed the roar in her ears. His heat enveloped her, chasing away the chills. She didn't know why he was here, but she knew she was safe.

After another minute, he put a hand under her chin and lifted her head so that she could see him more clearly. Then he put a finger to his lips, warning her to be quiet. He seemed as tense and primed for battle as she had been just seconds ago. Every muscle in his body felt coiled against hers. She could tell he was listening for sounds from inside her home though his gaze remained locked on her.

For an instant frozen in time, they stared at each other as strangers with bodies meeting for the first time.

The male scent of him triggered a deeply feminine reaction. Her breasts were crushed against the rigid wall of his chest. Their hearts hammered a riotous rhythm, pounding against each other.

Never had Sallie been more aware of the differences between male and female. His broad shoulders spanned inches beyond hers. The feel of his hard stomach and muscled thighs was indelibly printed against the softness of hers.

She and Cade had worked together, side-by-side, for the last five years, but they'd never crossed the line between professional and personal. Being forced to do it now, under such bizarre circumstances, had her senses reeling.

Stripped of her usual defenses, it was impossible to ignore the sheer male potency of him. Her skin tingled everywhere they touched. Cade shifted slightly and the movement heightened the awareness of body against body. Heat flooded through Sallie on a wave of erotic sensuality, shocking and scorching in its intensity.

His gaze probed so deeply that it stilled her breathing again. The brief flare of smoldering desire in his incredible eyes was flattering, frightening and totally unprecedented in their relationship.

Before her befuddled brain could arrive at feasible explanation for their reaction to each other, they heard a thud in the living room. There was grunting and cursing and the sound of some sort of skirmish. Then the front door slammed against the wall. Cade released her, heading into the house.

"Stay here!"

Another chill raced over her as she lost the heat of his body. Ignoring his order, she ran after him, snatching her robe from a chair as she passed through the bedroom. She shoved her arms through the sleeves and followed him into the darkened living room. Moving quickly toward a light switch, she flipped it to illuminate the room.

It was empty except for her and Cade, but the front door stood wide open. He went to the doorway and peered into the night.

"What in the world is going on?" she demanded, hating the raw, distraught sound of her own voice.

"Steven and I saw someone breaking into your house. We separated so that I could cover the balcony while he went around to the front. He must have surprised the guy when he tried to leave."

Steven Tanner was the security chief at Langden Industries. Cade owned the company, and she was his executive assistant. Neither man had ever visited her home. She couldn't imagine what had brought them here tonight.

"You saw someone breaking into my house?" she asked, following Cade to the door.

"Yeah," he said as he stepped off the small porch. "We called the police, but didn't know how long it would take them to respond." He strode down the sidewalk to the parking area of the condominium complex, surveying the surrounding area.

Sallie kept him in sight, but stayed hidden in the doorway. Her pale yellow nightgown and robe were sheer and nearly transparent. She didn't care to parade around where her neighbors might see. She lived in a quiet community where everyone respected each other's privacy, and she had no desire to make a spectacle of herself.

A stiff breeze whispered across her flesh, a norm for Dallas, even this late at night. The air was warm and balmy compared to the cool of her house, but it chilled her sweat-dampened skin. She crossed her arms over her chest and rubbed her forearms with hands that trembled. With a little more effort, she regained control over the rest of her quivering body.

Her attention stayed on Cade as he paced the sidewalk, and then headed back toward the house. He reached the porch at the same time Steven came jogging around the corner of the building.

"I lost him. He had a car parked on the other side of the complex. I couldn't even get a clear plate number," he added.

"It's dark, and he must know his way around," said Cade. "He caught us off guard, so there wasn't much we could do."

"You could explain to me exactly what's going on," she insisted huskily.

The men exchanged glances, but before they could reply, a police cruiser pulled into the parking lot, lights flashing. Sallie cringed, but was relieved that the policemen weren't using their sirens.

"I'll go talk to them," said Steven. "There's probably nothing more that can be done tonight."

Cade nodded and reentered the house, then closed the door. He immediately started searching her home.

It hadn't been that long since she'd left him at the office. He still wore the jeans and dress shirt he'd worn earlier, so he must have worked all evening. A glance at the clock showed just past twelve.

When she could trust her voice not to squeak, she asked, "What brought you here at midnight? And how did Steven get into my living room to run off the intruder?"

"There's not a lock Steven can't open," Cade explained as he came from her kitchen and headed back toward the bedroom. "We had an anonymous phone call warning us that one of our executive staff might be in danger. We drove over here to check on you and saw a man on your balcony. Can you tell if anything's missing?"

Sallie decided to postpone her interrogation until she had his full attention. Her gaze swept the living room, but the only thing out of place was a chair. She figured it got shifted during the scuffle, so she slid it back to its normal position.

A quick perusal of her desk assured her nothing important was missing. Her briefcase was locked, and her pocketbook still held her wallet with its usual contents, including the cash. Steven stepped back in the door and asked if there was any theft to report. She shook her head, and he left again.

Cade prowled through her house, and then returned to the living room. Sallie tightened the belt of her robe, but that didn't make her feel any less exposed. This was the first time her boss had ever stepped foot inside her home. It made her nervous. She watched intently as he roamed the room.

Cade had thick, dark hair, warm brown eyes and bronzed, golden skin. He had a lean, muscular build with broad shoulders and narrow hips. His good looks and easy charm made him a hit with most women, but had never been a factor in their working relationship.

Until a few minutes ago, they'd never been in a physically compromising position. A rush of heat coursed through her as she remembered the feel of being pressed so tightly against him. She quickly banished the thought. Gorgeous men like Cade Langden didn't get personally interested in plain women like her. For that, she'd be eternally grateful.

"Did you get a good look at this guy?" she asked.

"From a distance, he looked short and stocky."

He finally stopped searching and moved closer to her. His gaze lingered on her features, and she felt the unaccustomed wash of heat in her cheeks. Clenching her teeth, she willed the silly feminine reaction to subside.

"I'd say he's in good physical condition if he managed to outrun Steven."

"Do you think this is related to the trouble we're having at the plant?" she asked.

Langden's manufactured tractor engines. Until recently, they'd never had security problems, but there'd been trouble brewing of late.

"I'm guessing it's the same guy, since he called the office. What I can't understand is why he singled you out." His brows creased in a deep frown. "He didn't try to hurt you, so why break in here? What's he after that he thinks you might have at home?"

"I don't keep any important papers here."

"Maybe he just wants to up the ante a little," Cade growled, raking a hand through his hair. "He's not satisfied to cause trouble at the plant. He wants to get personal. He probably figured we'd be more alarmed with you as a target."

Sallie didn't like that suggestion at all or the worry etched on Cade's handsome features. "Do you think he's playing some kind of sick game with us?"

"It's hard to tell." His mouth tightened in an angry scowl. "He was probably wearing gloves, but we could get the place dusted for prints."

Sallie shook her head. She didn't want to involve the police any more than necessary. "I wasn't attacked and it doesn't look like anything was stolen. The police can't do anything about his vague threats, so there's not much reason to call them."

"I think it's time we filed a police report on the whole situation," said Cade, propping his fists on his hips. The action strained the fabric of his shirt across his broad chest. "This escalates a nuisance problem to breaking and entering."

Sallie nodded and shifted her gaze. Why was she suddenly so aware of Cade's chest? The very thought made her frown and bite her lip.

"In the meantime," said Cade, "I'll put a round-the-clock guard on you."

"No!" she all but screeched.

He quit pacing and stared at her. His sudden stillness convinced her that the harshly uncharacteristic tone had shocked him. She frowned at her lack of control and struggled for composure.

"No guards," she insisted. She'd spent the better part of her life in a gilded cage, and she refused to go back to that way of living. "I do not want a bodyguard."

"It wouldn't really be a bodyguard," Cade reasoned, his gaze a little too probing for comfort. "Just someone to watch for strangers."

"No." She shook her head back and forth. Agitated, she lifted both arms to shove her hair off her face, belatedly realizing it must be a wild mess. "I don't want someone watching every move I make, even if they are in our employ."

When she looked at Cade again, their gazes clashed. She saw a flash of something hot and purely masculine in his eyes. It made her pulse pound at an alarming rate. Too late, she realized that lifting her arms had also lifted the hem of her robe from mid-thigh to mid-bikini underwear. She promptly lowered her arms and cinched her robe more tightly at the waist.

Cade looked as shaken as she felt by the newly charged tension between them. He turned his head and crammed his hands into his back pockets. "Okay, if you don't want a bodyguard, at least let us install some electronic security."

She ignored the suggestion. "I have sturdy locks on the French doors as well as deadbolts. I don't know how anybody could get past them." Sallie felt proud of her firm, reasonable tone, considering her insides were quaking.

"The deadbolts couldn't have been locked. We saw him use something to open the regular lock, but he didn't have to force his way inside."

"I know the deadbolts were secure this morning."

"Maybe he was already inside the house today and took care of them himself," suggested Cade, his tone and expression grim. "Maybe the whole thing was a setup tonight, strictly for our benefit. Have you had any visitors? Repairmen? Delivery men? Or any women?"

"No, no one," said Sallie. She shivered and hugged her arms again. A chill ran down her spine at the thought of a stranger entering her home at will. It just didn't make sense.

"He just stopped at the end of my bed and mumbled something, then came in to the living room. I don't know why he came in here first. Do you think he was looking for something specific? "

"Good question. Maybe he was just scoping out your security system. It wouldn't hurt to install more security," said Cade, his dark eyes studying her intently. "Normal locks are no challenge to an experienced thief. Steven can do the work, and the company will foot the bill."

"I hate it," Sallie argued, feeling pressured. "I don't want to be a prisoner in my own home. I refuse to let anyone intimidate me to that level. I'll be more careful."

He made a sound of frustration and started to argue, but then Steven returned. He was of the same opinion and reiterated the need for additional security.

Sallie still stalled. She'd spent too many years locked behind state-of-the-art security systems. This was her home, and she didn't want it to become a fortress, but she did want to feel safe.

"How about letting me bring some equipment in to check for electronic bugs?" asked Steven. "This guy could have planted listening devices."

She shuddered again. That would be the worst invasion of privacy. The thought made her sick to her stomach. Maybe she shouldn't be too quick to rule out more security. "I'd be grateful if you would do that for me. There's no need to worry about it tonight, but I'd appreciate having it done as soon as possible."

"Why don't I stop by here before you leave for work tomorrow? I'll check for bugs. If you want, I can have the locks changed, too. Something with a code would be better than a regular key."

She hesitated, and Cade cajoled, "You're a whiz with numbers, Sallie. A code won't be a problem, so why not beef up your security? You don't want somebody coming in here whenever they please."

The idea of someone recording her private conversations had her rethinking her refusal. She nodded in agreement, feeling a deep conflicting of emotions as she did. She'd made a vow never to insulate herself behind a wall of security. The personal promise had stemmed from hard-learned lessons, yet her current situation warranted a hefty measure of common sense.

Glancing from Cade to Steven, she saw increasing concern in their eyes and realized her emotional struggle was apparent. Drawing on ever-crumbling reserves of control, she managed a more guarded expression.

Her gaze met Cade's for the space of several heartbeats. Tension pulsed between them, thick and fraught with unanswered questions. She shook her head in a barely perceptible movement, denying any desire to communicate her concerns.

He finally broke the uneasy silence. "It's late and it's been a long day. We all need some sleep. Would you like to get a motel room for tonight or call someone to spend the rest of the night with you?"

Sallie didn't know a soul she'd feel comfortable calling at midnight. "You don't think he'll come back, do you?"

They both shook their heads. Steven moved toward the door, but Cade hesitated. He continued to study her. "We've got things locked up now, so you should be safe.

And I can be back here in a matter of minutes if anything spooks you," he said. "Or I'll camp out on your sofa, if you want."

The suggestion nearly had her hyperventilating. Instead of calming her, his obvious concern made her feel edgy and agitated. She relived the numbing fear and the resulting surge of sensual alarm when he'd grabbed her earlier. Cade's efforts to protect her had scared her almost as much as the intruder.

She hated being afraid.

A surge of heat raced through her body, causing another rush of adrenaline as she remembered how it felt to be trapped under his weight. The roller coaster of emotions snapped her considerable control.

Picking up a throw pillow, she grasped it tightly and moved closer to him. "Just one more thing," she said, then swung the pillow wildly.

Thwap! She whacked his shoulder. It wasn't an attempt to hurt him, but to relieve some of her nerve-jangling tension.

"What the hell!" Cade stared at her as though she'd lost her mind.

"That's for scaring me witless tonight!"

A look of disbelief flashed across his face. "I didn't scare you on purpose," he insisted.

"You could have identified yourself before you slammed me against the wall!"

His eyes narrowed, his expression mirroring the belligerence of hers. "I tried, but you weren't listening. I didn't know where the intruder was or if he had a weapon. All I wanted to do was protect you."

Sallie frowned. He had a point, but she didn't want to think of him as her protector, either. "You should have made sure I knew who you were before you scared me even more."

"I tried to be gentle," he groused. "You're the one who went ballistic and started fighting like a wild woman."

Thwap! She hit him again at the reminder of how terrified she'd been. It felt good to have a physical release for all the pent-up emotion. Her loss of control was a throw back to her younger days, but the whole situation had her badly rattled.

"What was I supposed to do? Just stand there until you decided to explain yourself? I don't take kindly to being manhandled!"

Cade's voice grew tighter. "Then you damned well better learn to lock your doors. Or let us keep a guard outside."

They continued to glare at each other until Steven loudly cleared his throat. She'd been so caught up in her tirade that she'd almost forgotten his presence. Turning to glare at him, she noted a glimmer of amusement in his normally bland expression.

"You think it's funny?" she snapped. Her whole body trembled with anger—a delayed reaction to the scare she'd gotten. Somewhere in the back of her mind she realized the anger wasn't really directed at them, but she desperately needed an outlet for the frustration.

"Calm down," insisted Cade. "We're leaving. Don't launch an attack on Steven. He was only trying to help."

She wasn't in any mood to be chastised or pacified. "Then leave! Thank you for coming to my rescue, but please leave and let me get some sleep."

Cade flashed her another frown, but followed Steven onto the porch. He stood just outside the door and waited until she'd slammed and locked it. Sallie made sure he heard her secure the lock.

"Good night."

She heard his parting words and collapsed against the door, pressing her forehead against the cool panel. It took several minutes of slow, deep breathing to settle her pulse into a normal rhythm again. Then she slowly replayed the last half hour in her mind, like a kaleidoscope of rapidly changing emotions, and felt totally appalled by her behavior.

What in the world must they be thinking? She wondered with a groan of self-disgust. Normally so prim and proper, she'd acted like a total shrew, hysterical and uncontrolled. She could hardly believe her own actions. Hitting Cade. She'd hit Cade. He'd looked dazed. They probably thought her a lunatic.

It had been years since she'd lost her temper that way and never in front of them. Professional decorum was of utmost importance to her. She never let her personal feelings get the upper hand, rarely raised her voice, but tonight she'd gone spastic.

Groaning again, she shoved herself away from the door and walked across the room. Maybe if she went to bed, she'd wake up in the morning and find it was all a bizarre nightmare. Deep, dreamless sleep sounded like the perfect panacea right now.

Turning out the lights, she moved back into her bedroom and checked the locks on the French doors. It wasn't a surprise to find a chair propped against the frame to insure the doors couldn't be pried open again.

Slipping off her robe, she tossed it over the chair and then slid into bed. The sheets were cool, reminding her of the contrasting heat of Cade's big body. Every inch of him measured sexy, powerful male. Her boss was considered one of the most eligible bachelors in Texas. His wealth, intelligence and innate charm made him a favorite target for women with matrimony in mind.

Or, for women with just men on their mind.

Sallie had never been one of them. Any physical reaction to Cade's presence had always been tightly harnessed. Tonight's fiasco could only lead to trouble if she let herself dwell on it too much.

She didn't want to know how his body felt against hers, how the hard masculine angles fit so perfectly against softer feminine curves. She'd always had a certain feminine curiosity about him, but nurturing fantasies would be unbelievably stupid.

There was no special man in her life, and she'd had very few romantic relationships. As a vulnerable teenager, she'd trusted the wrong man with her heart, and he'd betrayed her. He'd been one of her dad's protégés, and had taught her an invaluable lesson. She didn't dare give her heart to a man who was driven to succeed. Men like her father who worked sixty-hour weeks and had little time to devote to serious relationships. Who had only heartache to offer the women who loved them.

Men like Cade.

Though older and wiser now, it still hurt to remember the humiliation of that first failed romance. Experience had taught her to be wary. She wanted to believe she wouldn't make the same mistake again, but she'd lost faith in her own judgment.

Forcing aside the depressing thoughts, Sallie belatedly remembered the friend who always offered unconditional love and comfort.

"They're gone now, Jas," she whispered sleepily. "You can come out from under the bed."

Chapter Two

It was the lace that drove him crazy, Cade decided, as his gaze drifted to Sallie's long, nylon clad legs. It was the tiny, tempting peeks at frilly feminine lace that made his pulse accelerate and kept his imagination running rampant.

Seated on the opposite side of his desk, she looked every inch the professional, wearing a very businesslike blue suit with just a scrap of lace visible at the slit of the skirt. That tiny ruffle had him mesmerized.

"Steven's on his way," she said, drawing his gaze upward. Her wide, hazel eyes were faintly questioning. Her perfectly modulated tone held cool detachment. "Do you want to wait on him before we discuss this report?"

"Might as well wait," Cade responded absently while his thoughts and gaze strayed to her lingerie again.

Over the years, he'd caught glimpses of colors ranging from the softest pastel to the boldest red, yet the frills were always concealed beneath very proper business attire. He'd noticed, but he hadn't given the subject much consideration.

Sallie's equally prim and proper demeanor didn't invite familiarity. Her attitude shouted "back off" to anyone who tried to get personal. At the same time, her very feminine, very sexy lingerie hinted at a passionate depth that intrigued him more every day. Lately, the lace and the lady were driving him nuts.

Last night had been packed with surprising revelations. Their unexpected intimacy had hotwired his senses. Not to mention how incredibly gorgeous she'd looked in that sheer nightgown, her tall, slender body and long, long legs enticing enough to excite any warm-blooded male.

Her ultra-feminine home had been another surprise, and when she'd lost her temper, she'd stirred his imagination to sheer fantasy.

He considered Sallie indispensable to Langden Industries. An engineer at heart, he'd had to work long and hard to develop his business skills, while she was a natural. Their strengths complemented each other. He'd offered her a partnership on several occasions, but she argued that she was satisfied with their working arrangement. She epitomized everything smart and sophisticated in their professional life, yet she'd always kept her private life carefully guarded.

For years, he'd been content with their professional relationship. There'd always been a tiny spark of attraction, but they'd never let it flame out of control. Over the past few months, that had changed. Now he wanted to trespass into territory considered off limits. He wanted to explore his growing attraction for her, yet she never offered him the slightest encouragement.

The intimacy they'd shared last night should have blasted the barrier between professional and personal, but this morning she was her usual no-nonsense, efficient self. She hadn't mentioned the incident at her home except to say Steven had been there earlier to install a new alarm system. She'd cut him off when he'd broached the subject on a more personal level.

A knock at the door interrupted his thoughts. Sallie rose and shifted the lace out of sight. Her sensible pumps made no sound in the plush carpet as she crossed the room, nor was there any irritating swish of fabric as she moved, just elegance and long-legged grace.

For some reason, her serene perfection irritated Cade.

He wanted to mess her up, he realized with a start. He wanted to pull the pins out of her severe hairstyle and comb it into a wild tangle with his fingers. He wanted to see the sparkle of gold in her dark blonde hair, just as he had last night. Then he wanted to peel off the oh-so-proper suit, layer by layer, until he unveiled all the lace. He wanted to explore every feminine inch of her.

The sheer force of desire knocked the breath out of him for a minute. It sent an arrow of heat shooting down to the center of his body, and made his muscles bunch with tension. Suddenly, his jeans were too tight, his nerves were raw and his blood ran hot.

What the hell was the matter with him? He'd never let a woman take control of his thoughts or blur his priorities. He liked women as well as the next guy, but business came first.

The unexpected death of his parents a few years back had left him and his brother on the brink of bankruptcy. Trey, the eldest, had worked tirelessly to save the ranch and keep a roof over their heads while he'd worked his way through college with odd jobs and scholarships. They'd made a pact to secure the family's financial future, and he was determined to hold up his end of the bargain.

So far, this year's peak season hadn't produced the projected revenue. He couldn't afford distractions right now. He had to get a grip and stop lusting after his assistant. There were more pressing issues in need of attention. If the problems at the plants escalated, it could put them way behind schedule. It would only take one really bad year to damage their reputation and threaten overall profits.

Sallie greeted Steven at the door and the two of them returned to take seats opposite his desk. Cade sucked in a deep, fortifying breath and forced himself to concentrate on Langden's problems. He leveled his gaze on the other man, avoiding eye contact with Sallie until his temperature had cooled.

"What's happening? Any new information?" he asked.

"I filed a report with the police this morning," said Steven, "but they admitted there's little they can do, especially about our internal problems. They did agree to have a squad make more regular runs past Sallie's complex."

Langden's had factories in Dallas and San Antonio. Several components of their tractor engines were produced in Dallas, and the finished engines were assembled in San Antonio. Although he was insistent about keeping their equipment in good repair, they'd suffered some suspicious breakdowns lately. The damages hadn't been serious, but they'd cost downtime and delays.

"So we're relatively sure these incidents are related?"

"That's my opinion."

"It sounds like someone with a grudge, but there haven't been any complaints of employee dissatisfaction. So who or what the hell's behind this?" Cade wanted to know.

"What about Don Carner, that bully you fired a few months ago?" asked Sallie. "He seemed the violent sort. Do you suppose he could be responsible?"

"We've been keeping a discreet eye on him after he made some threats against the company," Steven told her. "He's working with a shipping firm in Galveston and making good money. He seems content, so he's not a very likely suspect."

"Could it be someone trying to destabilize the business in a buyout attempt?" Sallie wondered aloud.

"Anything's possible," said Cade, "but we're financially sound, so there's little risk right now."

"Maybe someone's hoping to change that."

"It could be someone resents Langden's rapid growth in the area, or has a personal grudge against me or it's just a psycho bent on harassing a manufacturing company," he concluded.

"As far as I know," said Steven, "you've never had any complaints from environmental or conservation fanatics."

"Never," Cade insisted.

"Well, there's always greed and extortion," Sallie suggested. "Maybe someone's going to disable equipment, threaten us and then offer us protection for a hefty fee."

"You mean like organized crime?" Cade growled. He hated bullies of any kind. "There's been rumor of some area businesses having trouble, but not companies with their own security. I'm guessing it's a disgruntled employee or former employee."

"And he's either stupid or he wants us to get wise to him," Steven suggested. "The warning before the break-in at Sallie's was a deliberate taunt."

Cade threaded his fingers through his hair. "He's probably a mental deviant who gets his kicks by toying with us. If he gets any bolder, the taunting could escalate to violence, and somebody might get hurt."

As the men bounced around more possibilities, Sallie quietly studied each of them. They were alike in some ways, honest, hardworking and dependable. But they were very different in nature. Their reactions to the unknown threat highlighted the differences.

Steven remained detached and objective while Cade was openly emotional. The business and his employees elicited his passionate defense. He was one of the old guard who felt it his personal responsibility to protect everyone around him.

Four years ago, a powerful drug lord had threatened his sister-in-law's life. Cade and his brother, Trey, had worked closely with law enforcement officials to protect Jillian.

That's the only time Sallie could remember him taking extra time off work. She'd always admired that protective trait, even though it made him more demanding and driven to succeed. She just hoped he'd keep his protective tendencies focused on the company instead of her.

"What do you think, Sallie?"

She blinked and dragged her attention back to the conversation. The men had been discussing the best way to handle employee concerns.

"I think you need to have a meeting to address the issue," she replied. "We have intelligent, capable people working for us. Give them the facts. Otherwise, there'll be rumors and speculation that could add to our problems."

Both men nodded their agreement.

"You might offer a reward to anyone with information," Steven added.

"Yeah," said Cade. "The employees are likely to hear more than we do. There'll be a lot of unfounded rumors, but it could offer us a lead or two."

"Right now, we don't even have a clue, do we?" she asked.

"Nothing in regard to the factory," said Steven. "I did find electronic bugs in your house, though. The police wanted me to send them to their labs, but they're notoriously slow and overworked. I left one with them and sent the other two to a private lab. I'm hoping we'll get lucky with a fingerprint or something, but I'm not counting on it."

Sallie felt all the blood drain from her face. A sickening queasiness settled in her stomach. The thought of someone invading her privacy to such an extent made her physically ill. A wave of fear followed and that made her angry. Curling her fingers into fists, she fought to keep a level tone.

"You found three listening devises in my house?"

Steven nodded, his expression tight. "One each in the living room, the kitchen and the bedroom. Maybe that's why he be slipped into your house last night. He could have been checking his equipment or just planting it."

The unmitigated gall. "So that's how..." she began aloud, then immediately regretted the slip of tongue. Abrupt silence followed the aborted statement.

Cade stared at her and prodded, "That's how what?"

Sallie flashed an annoyed glance at him. She didn't want to discuss the issue, but she knew he wouldn't be satisfied until she clarified her slip. "I was getting some nuisance phone calls, so I had my phone number changed."

Cade's expression darkened. "That didn't stop the calls?"

"No."

"Did you report the calls to the police?"

"Yes, but there's nothing they can do. They suggested I change the number, get caller ID and screen my calls through the answering machine. I'm doing all that now."

"Why the hell didn't you mention this last night?"

Her temper flared, but she put a damper on it and forced herself to remain calm. She hadn't mentioned it last night because she didn't want to discuss it. The calls were more embarrassing than threatening.

"I turned the answering machine tapes over to the police, but the calls aren't obscene or threatening. They're just considered nuisance calls, and I think the police are beginning to consider me a nuisance for complaining."

"Then what does the guy say? I assume it's a guy."

"The voice is electronically altered, but it sounds like a man."

"So?" Cade demanded. "Do you know the guy? What does he say if he's not obscene or threatening? Does he just ask you out? Harass you for a date? There are laws against stalking, you know."

"I don't know him, he doesn't ask me out, and he doesn't meet the criteria for a stalker," she insisted in frustration, then instantly calmed her tone again. "For some reason, I'm just a target for his calls right now. The police think he'll get bored and stop calling if I ignore him long enough."

Cade and Steven exchanged looks that made Sallie chew her lip in irritation. She didn't like the silent, utterly male communication. She had no desire to become their main security project. That's exactly why she hadn't mentioned the problem in the first place. She needed to handle it herself.

"The phone company has a privacy option you can use to block unwanted calls," said Steven. "You have to sign up for it and pay a monthly fee, but that might be a good way to discourage this guy."

She knew about the system and had already looked into it. Each new restriction threatened more of her personal freedom, but independence had to take a back seat to peace of mind now that her home had been invaded.

"I've already ordered it."

Cade held her gaze for a long time. "We can't rule out a stalker. Someone might be stalking you, but causing trouble at the plant to cover his tracks."

"It doesn't make sense," she argued. "There's absolutely no one that I know who'd do such a thing."

"Maybe it's not someone you know," added Steven. "There are a lot of lunatics in the world with obsessive tendencies. It could be someone you know casually who's gone off the deep end."

Sallie shook her head in dismissal of the idea.

Cade didn't dismiss the idea as quickly. "Hopefully we'll get to the bottom of both problems soon. Until we know more, the new coded locks on your doors should keep you safe. Steven can run another electronic scan anytime you feel the need."

"Thanks. I hope it's not necessary. The police seem to think it's a prankster who'll get bored and quit bothering me." The whole situation made her uncomfortable, so she changed the subject. "Did you want to go over this personnel report now?"

Cade glanced at his watch. "I've got that conference call with the San Antonio office in a few minutes. Why don't you and Steven go over the records and see if there's anyone else who might have reason to cause us trouble."

"You want a complete background on any employee who might be suspect?" asked Steven.

"A complete on everyone. I know it'll take more time, but I'd rather be thorough. I don't want this guy slipping through the cracks."

His dismissive tone had her and Steven rising from their seats. After brief farewells, they headed for the door.

Sallie knew Cade didn't need anything else, yet she felt him watching their exit with unusual intensity. Just before leaving the room, she shot a glance at him over her shoulder. Their gazes met, and a quiver coursed through her at the tension she saw in his handsome features.

She'd changed the subject when he tried to discuss the strange intimacy they'd shared last night, but the hot, probing look in his eyes told her he wasn't going to let it go. His look issued a challenge that could seriously complicate her life as well as their working relationship.

She didn't realize that her breath was trapped in her lungs until Steven closed the door and spoke to her. She dragged in air and determinedly put Cade out of her mind. They'd both been under a lot of strain lately. There had never been anything sexual between them, and she wanted it to stay that way. This unexpected tension was unacceptable.

It took over an hour to review the personnel files. They compared notes on anyone who'd ever filed a complaint against the company, and then Steven went to his own office to start background checks for current and past employees. Sallie got busy with her own morning routine.

Just after noon, Cade opened the door between their offices and approached her desk. He perched on the edge, as he'd done hundreds of times over the years, but this time she felt his proximity with every fiber of her being. Warmth crept under her skin and her nerves sizzled. Instinct warned her that he wanted to discuss last night and it caused instant panic.

"I gave Steven information about all the former employees who might hold a grudge," she spoke quickly, forestalling whatever he wanted to say.

"Thanks," he said, and then her phone rang just as he started to speak again. His forehead creased in annoyance, but she quickly lifted the receiver.

"It's Steven. He says he's ready to fly you to San Antonio." The company owned a small helicopter for easy travel between their two plants. "He says you should probably leave right now if you want to be back this evening."

"Tell him I'll meet him in the lobby," said Cade. After she'd relayed the message and hung up the phone, he asked, "Want to come with us?"

Normally she would have welcomed a chance to get out of the office on such a sunny spring day, but she wasn't feeling anywhere near normal. She needed a little time and distance from her boss.

"I'd better take a rain check," she replied without looking directly at him. Still, she felt the intensity of his gaze on her. "I really need to get some work done here."

A heavy silence fell between them. Sallie risked a glance at him, but she couldn't maintain eye contact for more than a couple seconds. The penetrating look in his eyes made her want to squirm, and she hated the feeling. Whatever he had on his mind, she hoped he kept it there.

"Okay."

He didn't sound pleased, but neither did he argue. Relief washed over her as soon as he moved away from her desk. Suddenly, she could breathe again.

"I'll see you Monday, but Steven and I will be back tonight, so don't hesitate to call if you have any problems at your place."

"Thanks, I'll do that," she lied, wondering if she should cross her fingers behind her back.

He mumbled, "yeah, right," and headed for the door. The comment brought a smile to her lips and instantly improved her disposition. She didn't want anyone thinking she needed protecting. He and Steven didn't have to waste time worrying about her. She had an obsessive need to maintain control of her life. It stemmed from too many years of being smothered by her father's security forces.

Lunch consisted of a sandwich at her desk, and the rest of the afternoon dragged, even for a Friday. Despite attempts to work, her thoughts kept drifting back to last night. She remembered every tiny detail of the volatile encounter between her and Cade, but mostly the way he'd made her feel so feminine and needy. He'd tapped into a core of sensuality she'd kept a tight lid on for years.

The subtle changes in their relationship alarmed her. It had to stop. She didn't want her professional life disrupted. Her work was her security, both financially and emotionally.

At six o'clock, Sallie joined the rest of the staff as they headed home for the weekend. Within a half hour, she'd closed the door of her house while simultaneously dropping her purse and kicking off her shoes. She was exhausted, and it was a treat to be home.

The invasion of her privacy last night had made it hard to regain a sense of safety and security. It had been a challenge to relax, but during the long, sleepless hours, she'd vowed not to let any lowlife thug destroy her love for her home.

She breathed in the mingled scents of potpourri and heaved another sigh of pleasure. After struggling out of her suit jacket, she tugged the blouse from the waist of her skirt. It was hot and she wanted cool air on her flesh.

Jasper, a multi-colored, mixed-breed cat, started his affectionate stroking of her ankles while purring a loud welcome.

"Hi there, kitty cat. Did you miss me today?" she asked, lifting the big, ugly cat into her arms.

He had to be the product of Mother Nature in the throes of a temper tantrum. His coloring was split down the middle of his body, half white, half black. A splash of dark color under his nose gave him an Adolph Hitler style of mustache.

"But you have fine, sleek fur," she praised while rubbing her face against the silky softness of his head. She'd adopted him from the local humane society.

He only had one other little-bitty flaw, an aversion to men. Even the scent of a man had him hiding under her bed. As a guard cat, he was totally useless, but he was also the only pet she'd ever had in her life. She adored him.

The ringing of the phone interrupted their affectionate greetings. It shattered the calm, and Sallie tensed with dread. Her hold on Jasper grew so tight that he yowled and jumped from her arms.

When the phone pealed a second time, she eased closer to it, holding her breath. After the fourth ring, her voice filled the tense silence with the outgoing message. Then she went rigid with tension as the deep, muffled voice spoke.

"Welcome home, honey," it said. "Have you kicked off those high heels and stripped off that pretty blue power suit? Make yourself comfortable and pour yourself a glass of wine. You deserve it. You didn't get much sleep last night, did you? Pamper yourself tonight. Mmm...wish I could be with you," he added in an intimate whisper.

Then the line went dead.

All the fine hairs on her body prickled with alarm. As always, the caller knew what she was wearing. Her gaze flew to the window, but no one could see through the closed blinds. He could have seen her anywhere at anytime today, at the office, on her way home or just outside the house. It gave her the creeps, even though his messages weren't obscene or threatening.

And he knew about last night! Had he been watching her house or had he actually been inside it? Had he been coming and going on a regular basis? Had he planted the listening devices? Was he harassing her because of Langden's or causing trouble for the company because of her? Who was he and why was he harassing her?

Legs trembling so badly that she could hardly stand, Sallie dropped into a chair. What a nightmare! She closed her eyes while fighting off a wave of panic. Jasper jumped into her lap, cuddling close to comfort.

Her unknown caller had been hounding her for weeks, but now she knew how he'd thwarted her attempts to be rid of him. He'd listened to private conversations and heard her give her new number to her friends and family.

The phone company had assured her that she'd have more privacy beginning on Monday. Then all calls from untraceable sources would be blocked. Steven had gotten rid of the bugs. Maybe now she'd get some peace.

She deeply resented the fact that some psychopath had the ability to destroy her peace of mind. The calls made her feel vulnerable and that made her furious. He'd invaded her privacy on two levels now, and she wanted it stopped.

There was no reason for anyone to harass her. She was single, lived alone except for Jas, and rarely dated. She wasn't beautiful, nor was she gregarious or popular. She preferred a quiet lifestyle. There was only one rejected man in her past, and he'd moved on to greener pastures.

The phone rang again, the sound sizzling along her nerves like lightning across water. Jas sensed her anxiety and pressed closer. She listened with bated breath as the ringing ceased, her message played and a male voice came over the wire.

Chapter Three

"Sallie, it's Cade. If you're there, pick up."

Relief surged through her, bringing warmth to chase away the chill. She eased Jasper off her lap and reached for the receiver, but her hand shook so badly that she had to take a deep, calming breath before responding.

"Hi, Cade, what's happening?" she asked, keeping her voice under tight control. She didn't want him to guess how desperate she was at the moment for contact with a normal human being.

"Were you busy?"

The tremors had stopped quaking through her body. "No, I just got home."

"Any plans for this evening?"

The question was so unexpected, it distracted her from the problem caller. Cade had her full attention.

"I planned a quiet evening," she replied, even though spending the evening alone had lost all appeal.

"Could you meet me in about an hour?"

Her brows furrowed in a frown. Cade was a workaholic, but he'd never called her back downtown after

Cade's Challenge

she'd left for the day. Still, it beat staying home and risking further harassment by phone.

"You want me to come to the office?"

"No. I need a date."

[...] skipping again, her frown [...] of female friends, so why her [...] he didn't have plans for

[...] he drawled in a patently

[...] later," he promised. "Do you

[...] she thought. She owned one [...] member the last time she'd [...] more to silk and satin. She [...] against her skin.

"I have some jeans. Why?"

A teasing, slightly challenging note entered Cade's voice. "I want to take you honky-tonkin'."

The phrase was familiar enough, but not the specifics. Sallie wasn't sure exactly what honky-tonkin' meant, but she was certain the reason she'd never done it was that she wouldn't like doing it. As far as she knew, Cade wasn't one to frequent bars either.

"I need jeans to do this?"

"We need to blend into the scenery. Jeans, boots, hats. You can wear the whole works if you want."

45

Jeans and boots were normal attire for him. Sallie leaned toward designer labels. For her, western attire was quite a deviation from the norm.

"Where are you going?" His invitation was so out of character that it made her wary. Intrigued, but wary.

He named a bar she'd never heard of called the Tumbleweed Tavern. He suggested she take a cab since it was located in a rough part of the city.

"I'll drive you home," he added.

Indecision warred within Sallie, a rarity for her. The invitation was tempting, but a little too personal for comfort. On the other hand, she knew he couldn't be seriously interested in her on a personal level. Not when he could have his pick of any number of beautiful women.

Balanced on the fine line between professional and personal, she hedged. "Does this place serve food?" Her stomach was already grumbling, and she didn't want to drink her dinner.

"Probably, but I won't guarantee you'll like it," he said. "You might want to eat something before you come."

His teasing response had her relenting. This was the Cade she knew and understood. "How soon should I be there?"

"I'm leaving my apartment in a few minutes. It'll take me half an hour, and I'll save a stool for you," he teased. "Just don't talk to any strangers and don't stand me up."

Sallie doubted he'd ever been stood up in his life, and she'd never known him to mix business with pleasure. This outing had to have something to do with the problems at Langden's. Maybe he had a lead and didn't want to discuss it over the phone.

Except for his family, everything else in his life was put on hold until business matters were settled. She just couldn't imagine how a place called Tumbleweed Tavern would relate to business.

Evidently, Cade had a plan and it included her.

"I'll be there," Sallie promised, then said goodbye.

She replaced the receiver and turned her attention to Jasper. "Well, it seems I'm going honky-tonkin' with my boss. Let's go see if I can still wear those jeans."

As she passed through the living room to the bedroom, her gaze scanned all the warm, homey furnishings she loved so much. She'd chosen a blend of soft pastels with cream carpet and draperies. Even more importantly, she'd paid for every single item, from the largest pieces of furniture to the smallest decorative touches. The pride she found in that accomplishment never ceased to boost her spirits.

She wasn't materialistic, so just owning nice things didn't give her the satisfaction. She'd grown up surrounded by beautiful, expensive belongings. But they hadn't meant half as much as the modest things she'd provided for herself.

The intense pleasure came from making her own decisions, from choosing what she thought was best for herself and being totally in control of her surroundings. The pride came from a hard-won sense of independence.

Her bedroom décor included varying shades of blue, lavender and purple. The carpet was a sculptured mix of all three colors, the drapes and matching bedclothes blended hues of lavender and the furniture was a rich, warm walnut.

Opposite her bed, at an angle from the French doors, was a huge, walk-in closet with circular racks for clothing. She loved clothes, and although a lot of her wardrobe consisted of business suits, she'd been raised to believe a woman needed specific clothes for specific occasions.

Tonight it was jeans. In a few minutes, she'd slipped into them, smiling when she had to suck in her stomach to pull up the zipper. Unlike most women, she was delighted that her hips were finally getting broader.

Most of her life she'd suffered the insecurity of feeling too tall, too thin and totally unattractive. Now she welcomed the maturing fullness of her figure. She was still a long way from voluptuous, but age had brought great improvement.

"What do you think, Jas? Are they scandalously tight or just fashionably snug?"

A slow feline yowl was the only response from her pet. He'd made himself comfortable on her bed and watched with narrow-eyed interest.

Sallie found a red silk tank top and put it on under a sheer red and white striped shirt that buttoned up the front and knotted at the waist. She liked the effect. The slim fit of the jeans and the fullness of the shirt gave her a shapelier image.

She didn't own a pair of boots and her sandals didn't go too well with the western image, so she settled on loafers. Feeling really daring, she slipped her feet into them without stockings. Her mother would be appalled, and the thought brought a wider smile to her lips.

"I don't know about the hair, Jas," she said, talking to her furry companion as she brushed her shoulder-length hair. She'd taken the pins from her chignon and didn't want to pull it up again. It was shining-clean and the ends curled just enough to give it shape, so she decided to leave it alone.

"I'll just let it all hang down," she added, feeling really risqué.

Jasper probably didn't understand the importance of living on the edge, she thought, her eyes sparkling as she retouched her makeup. Unbelievable as it seemed, an impromptu date with her boss was the most reckless thing she'd done in years.

A tiny frown marred her reflection when she recalled her last reckless fling, but she swiftly buried the memory. She was older now, more confident and a whole lot wiser.

༄༅༅༄

Cade settled into a booth at the Tumbleweed Tavern so that he had a good view of the entrance. He wanted to catch Sallie as soon as she came in the door or she might turn around and walk back out when she got a look at the place.

It was a dive, and it stunk. If he'd known how bad it was, he wouldn't have asked her to join him. He'd found a table in the section marked non-smoking, but the smoke wasn't following the rules. There was a good-sized crowd for so early in the evening, and the noise level was steadily rising.

A country and western band played at one end of the long room on a small stage behind an even smaller dance floor. There were no urban cowboys here, just genuine rednecks and what looked like a group of rodeo entertainers.

He'd be willing to bet Sallie had never stepped inside a place like this, but he could be wrong. For some reason, not knowing was like a splinter under a fingernail. It just kept smarting. They'd shared plenty of business dinners and traveled together on occasion, but always first class.

She seemed completely at ease with their wealthy clients and at the finest restaurants. She never talked about her upbringing, but her flawless manners and impeccable taste indicated a privileged background. He felt sure she'd been raised in the lap of luxury.

The Tumbleweed Tavern was far from luxurious. The olive green, cracked vinyl seats squeaked every time he shifted his weight. The stained Formica tabletop was decorated with cigarette burns and bottle rings. Its only additional adornment was a napkin holder with salt and pepper shakers.

Cade took a swallow of beer and enjoyed the tart taste. He was bone tired and badly in need of sleep, but restless energy kept him from relaxing. The same restlessness had plagued him for months. It wasn't just his self-imposed celibacy, but Sallie and his escalating desire for her.

Always a man of action, he'd learned to deal with problems head-on once he'd pinpointed the source. His assistant was a whole different story. She wasn't like any woman he'd ever dated. He'd reached the ripe old age of thirty-two without having to beg for any woman's attention. Women chased him because he'd never had the time or freedom to do the chasing. Most of his past relationships had involved career-minded women who were equally ambitious and had no interest in long-term commitment.

Sallie wanted to ignore the chemistry. He was sure of that, just as sure as he was that it should be explored. There had to be a way to do it without alienating her or destroying their working relationship.

Shifting his gaze from a careful study of the customers to regular glances at the entrance, Cade's smile slowly widened as he anticipated her reaction to this place. He didn't have long to wait, but he didn't catch her expression because his eyes were feasting on the rest of her.

Damn, she was hot. Why hadn't he anticipated that? His body tightened as all that restless energy shifted to his lap. She not only owned a pair of jeans, it looked like they'd been made just for her long, slim legs and gently rounded hips. The blouse she'd paired them with was an enticing bit of fabric that accentuated the shape of her breasts.

The thought knocked the breath from his lungs in a sharp rush. He groaned, and then noticed that several of the bar patrons had taken an interest in her, too. He'd seen it happen a lot. Her elegance and willowy grace coupled with a touch-me-not air of indifference challenged men on the most elemental level.

For a long while, it had amused him to watch men fall victim to her unpretentious beauty. Now it just made him testy. She seemed oblivious to her effect on the male species. If he didn't intercede, they'd be tripping over each other to get closer.

Making his way across the room, Cade swiftly discouraged anyone intent on waylaying her. "Forget it," he growled at one cowboy who'd started toward Sallie with a gleam in his eyes. He passed several men straining their necks and shot them looks of warning.

When she finally caught sight of him, their gazes met, and Cade saw just a tiny flicker of relief in her eyes. He offered her a reassuring smile and lengthened his stride.

"So this is a honky-tonk," her soft, conspiratorial whisper greeted him as he reached her side. Her scent managed to penetrate the foul smells of the bar and tease him with its clean, fresh sweetness.

"A genuine, no-frills, redneck honky-tonk," he assured her, slipping an arm around her waist. He tucked her close to his side and guided her back to the relative isolation of the corner booth. It felt good to hold her, even briefly, and feel the rub of her body against his.

When lecherous eyes strained for a better look, he shielded her from view, feeling territorial. The emotional reaction caught him unaware and his jaw tightened. He wasn't the possessive, territorial type. So why the hell did he feel that way with Sallie?

"Sorry," he apologized after they were seated on opposite sides of the booth. "I didn't realize how rough this place was. I expected an upscale saloon with yuppies and urban cowboys. Once I got here, it was too late to change plans."

She gave him a tight smile. "I'm not too familiar with the wild side, but I think I can handle it for a while."

Cade's face creased in a grin. The ever-present glitter of amusement in his eyes suggested a laid-back, easygoing nature, but Sallie knew they hid a powerfully intense, success-driven man who allowed little time for relaxation.

Normally clean-shaven, his five o'clock shadow made him look darker and a little bit dangerous. "Did you forget to shave or are you in disguise?"

The glitter in his eyes intensified as he stroked his chin. "I wanted to blend with the crowd."

They studied each other intently for a few minutes. Then Sallie broke the silence with a typically straightforward question. "Why are we here?"

"I'll get to that, but first, would you like something to eat or drink? I don't think they carry your favorite wine."

She glanced at the bottle in front of him. "I'll have what you're having."

He arched a brow in surprise. "You like beer?"

"I doubt it." She'd never tasted it, but was feeling reckless. Not reckless enough, however, to drink anything out of a glass in this place. "There's only one way to find out."

Cade chuckled. "Why not be really brave and order something to eat?"

She'd eaten some yogurt at home, but still felt hungry. "What do you suppose the chances are of getting something safe and edible?"

"It might be possible. The waitress said the hamburgers are flame-broiled and packaged chips should be okay."

"That's what you're having?" At his nod, Sallie said, "I'll have the same."

Cade motioned for the waitress and gave their order, then sat back to have a good look at his companion. He liked her hair down. It looked soft and free of styling goop, with a healthy shine. At the office, he rarely saw a hair out of place. Tonight, it framed her face with sensuous softness, enhancing her eyes.

He'd always thought her eyes were her loveliest feature. They were a shade of gray-green that sometimes reflected green and sometimes looked more blue. They were big and bright and alive with intelligence.

"So what sort of business are we here to conduct?"

"I got another anonymous phone call. Some guy offered information about the trouble at the plant. I mentioned a reward today at the staff meeting in San Antone, and then repeated it for our Dallas plant. I had a call within an hour."

"Someone's really enjoying all this anonymity, aren't they?" she grumbled. "So why here? And how can he earn a reward if he doesn't identify himself?"

"He didn't want to risk being seen near the plant, so he chose a place on this side of town. I guess he plans to introduce himself and collect his money."

"And you immediately thought to invite me along," she said, deadpan.

Cade chuckled. She had a wicked sense of humor that had always delighted him. "There's a catch."

"I should have guessed. What else is involved?"

"Once we get the name of our malcontent, I want to go back to the office and search the personnel files. I could do it myself, but you're more familiar with those files."

Sallie nodded in understanding. He knew she'd be more comfortable if their time together was work related.

For the next few minutes, he caught her up-to-date on the meeting in San Antonio. There hadn't been any problems in that plant, so there were still no clues as to who was behind the ones in Dallas.

Their waitress reappeared, plopping both food and beer on the table in front of them. The harried woman was gone again before Sallie could even say thanks.

"At least the service is fast," she said.

Their sandwiches were served on clean paper plates, the buns looked fresh, and the meat smelled delicious.

"Mmm...not bad," said Cade after his first bite.

Her heart tripped at the sound he made. It reminded her of the frightening phone call earlier and sent a quiver of alarm down her spine. She stiffened, and then quickly admonished herself for the surge of panic.

"When and how is this man supposed to approach you?" she asked. "Do you have any idea who he is?"

"He refused to give his name, but he said he'd recognize me and make the contact. We're supposed to bump into each other by accident about nine o'clock near the men's restroom."

"Well I guess that restricts my participation."

"Uh-huh, unless you're feeling really adventurous."

Sallie had no intention of venturing near the men's restroom, so the subject was moot. She took a bite of her sandwich. It tasted really good, and she was hungry, so she enjoyed another bite.

"Judging by the sensation you caused when you walked in the door, there's not much hope of you sneaking into the john unnoticed," Cade continued after a couple of minutes of silence. "Your honky-tonk image is quite a variation from your business persona."

He paused briefly, and then continued in a low, challenging tone. "I think I'm in lust."

The wicked gleam in his eyes had Sallie rolling hers. He loved trying to shock her or get a rise out of her. From the earliest days of their working relationship, they'd shared a unique rapport. He teased, and she remained totally immune to his charm. She'd be stupid to put much stock in his sudden declaration of interest, even though it brought a flood of warmth under her skin.

Reluctant to let him draw her into a personal discussion, she took a sip of her beer and ignored the comment. "Did this mystery man give you any clue to his identity?" she asked, attempting to steer the conversation back on track.

Cade's eyes gleamed with unholy pleasure. "Changing the subject, Sallie?"

"It seemed the smart thing to do," she drawled, her gaze locking with his over the top of her beer bottle.

"Coward."

That one word, issued in a velvety smooth tone, sent an erotic little shiver along her nerves. He wanted to discuss whatever was developing between them. She wanted to ignore it. It wasn't worth the risk of permanently altering their relationship.

"I pick my battles carefully."

"And I'm not worthy of the effort?" His huskily spoken question was different now and entirely personal.

"Your game isn't," she corrected softly. It was her way of telling him to back off. She'd become an expert at keeping men at arm's length, and knew how to cool the most ardent advances with no more than a chilly look or a few succinct words.

Cade thrived on challenges, and so did she, on a professional level. But she didn't want anyone challenging her on a personal level. Her private life was just that, private. She intended to keep it that way.

His tone took on an edge. "You think I'm playing games?"

"I think we need to worry about one problem at a time," she insisted. "The threat to Langden's takes priority."

Cade frowned and looked like he wanted to argue, but he dropped the subject. When he lifted his bottle and took a swallow of beer, her gaze locked on his lips. A shiver of sensation coursed over her as she watched his mouth, so she reached for her own bottle and took a long, steadying drink. She decided it might be a good idea to concentrate on her food.

After they'd finished their meal, her control had reasserted itself, and she spoke again. "What are we supposed to do with ourselves until our mystery man appears?"

"Real honky-tonk heroes get steadily drunk, dance a lot or start fights," Cade told her.

Sallie grimaced. She'd never been drunk in her life. Her only experience with dancing was of the ballroom variety. She'd never instigated or been involved in a fight, so her options were really limited.

"I guess I could drink another beer."

Cade laughed, a deep husky sound that reverberated between them. "So you like the beer?" he asked, motioning for the waitress to bring them two more bottles.

"It's pretty disgusting, actually," she declared, scrunching her nose in distaste. "But I've heard it's an acquired taste."

"How many do you figure you have to drink to acquire it?"

"Too many to make the effort, I'm sure," she decided. "But I guess I can sip another one for a while."

"Nurse."

"Pardon?"

"You don't sip a beer, your nurse it."

"We're talking beer-drinker's lingo?"

"Yeah."

"Okay," Sallie conceded. "I can nurse it."

"That's the spirit. You need to lighten up a little."

She gave his casual remark serious consideration. "Why do you say that?"

"I don't know," he said. "It just seems like you need some fun in your life."

"Fun?" She wasn't certain that anything she'd done in her adult life could be called fun. Even as a child, her activities had been carefully orchestrated. She enjoyed a variety of hobbies now, but didn't think he'd qualify any of them as fun.

"Just plain fun," Cade explained in an exasperated tone. "Things like playing ball, shooting pool, horseback riding or skinny dipping. Especially the skinny dipping," he added with a wicked gleam in his eyes.

The mental image his words created made her skin tingle and her nipples tighten. She quickly banished the wayward thoughts. Her eyes flashed with annoyance as they met his over the bottle. She'd die before admitting she'd never done any of those things. It was a pointless conversation, anyway.

He grinned and saluted her with his beer bottle in a blatant attempt to rattle her composure.

"Care to dance?"

Sallie's eyes narrowed at the invitation, and she didn't bother to disguise her mistrust. Cade might seem like a carefree guy to most of the world, but she knew he didn't do anything without serious thought and consideration.

"I don't know how," she declared flatly, and then took a big swallow of beer. She hoped he'd accept the refusal.

He didn't.

"I've seen you dance plenty of times."

"Ballroom stuff. Not what they're doing." She nodded toward the dance floor.

"I'll teach you."

"And what if I don't want to learn?"

"Humor me," he drawled, his expression daring. "We have half an hour or so to wait, and I like to dance."

Sallie glanced around the room, feeling pressured. Surely there was someone else he could ask to dance. There were several other couples doing some sort of line dance on the tiny floor. The number of women in the bar seemed to have increased since she'd entered, yet none of them looked single or in search of a partner.

"You're the only candidate," he insisted, reading her thoughts. "It's not safe to pick up strange partners these days, you know."

"I really don't care to learn whatever they're doing."

"It's the boot-scootin' boogie," he explained. "But we can wait for a slow song."

Sallie studied him thoughtfully. She knew it had been several months since his last relationship disintegrated. He was rarely without someone special in his life, but he didn't have to chase women. They always came willingly. There were several vying for his attention right now.

For some reason, he'd been slow in choosing a new lover. He might be longing for feminine company. She had no intention of becoming a stand-in playmate, but the music was tempting.

"I can probably manage a slow dance," she finally announced.

He amazed her by throwing back his head and roaring with laughter. She frowned, genuinely confused and a little hurt. "Why is that so funny?"

He shook his head in disbelief. "Because it took you so damn long to decide. Have you ever done an impulsive thing in your life? Even under the influence of alcohol? You think too much, and I'm not used to having to beg someone for a dance. You need to unwind a little and get rid of some inhibitions."

It was Sallie's turn to shake her head. "No, thank you." She wanted control of everything around her, always. She might be the most organized schedule-slave he'd ever known, but that didn't bother her a bit.

When a deep frown replaced Cade's smile, she wondered where his thoughts had drifted. Did he think her need for control was boring and cowardly? She'd outgrown the adolescent desire to be daring, uninhibited and adventurous. The price for that sort of lifestyle was way too high.

For a couple of minutes they were both quiet while they finished their beers and studied each other more intently. Sallie wondered what the greater risk would be, meeting with an anonymous snitch or letting the boss take her in his arms again.

Chapter Four

"Come on," said Cade, rising and reaching a hand to her. "Let's go battle the masses for a piece of the dance floor."

Sallie accepted his outreached hand. His grip was firm and reassuring as he guided them through a sea of strangers. The bar was getting more crowded and the air staler by the minute. She hoped they didn't have to wait much longer to make contact with the mystery man.

As the band played a slow ballad, Cade took her in his arms. He slid both his hands around her waist to lock at the small of her back, so she flattened her palms on his chest. It was rock hard, the cotton of his shirt a fragile sheath for the coiled steel of masculine muscle.

His virile heat engulfed her, causing warmth to steal over her body. Her pulse leapt, and kept picking up speed as the warmth intensified. Every tiny nerve went haywire, electrifying her to painful awareness of their physical contact.

The fierce reaction to the feel of Cade's hard body shook her to the core. Everywhere they touched the sensations grew more powerful. With the crush of bodies on the tiny dance floor, it was impossible to distance herself. She shifted slightly, but he drew her still closer.

Sensual chaos reigned as they moved to the throbbing beat of the music. Her breasts tingled, her nipples tightening at the contact with his chest. Shocked by the swift, unexpected response, she prayed he couldn't feel the involuntary reaction.

As their thighs and bellies rubbed together, her stomach muscles clenched, and she felt an unfamiliar trembling in her legs. In a useless effort to hide her reactions, she laid her face in the curve of his shoulder and gave up any hope of rational conversation.

Cade was no help. He seemed perfectly content to have her draped against him, going so far as to slide his hands up her arms and then back down in a slow, sensual caress that created more havoc on her control.

Sallie supposed he was used to the erotic feel of masculine and feminine bodies rubbing against each other. She was not. She occasionally danced with business associates, but she'd never felt this kind of response.

Up close, the smell of him was equally disturbing as she inhaled a mixture of man and spicy musk. His scent flowed through her like warm honey, seeping into her subconscious to a purely feminine place she'd kept hidden and protected for a very long time.

She allowed herself to bask in the sensations for just a few minutes. One song ended and another began, but Cade showed no interest in releasing her. The slow, torturous brush of body against body continued, making Sallie's heart thud painfully in her chest.

"You going to sleep on me?" he prodded, softly, huskily.

His mouth was so close to her ear that she felt his heated breath whisper into her body and shiver down her spine. Even his voice seduced. His tone was as thick with slumberous sensuality as her thoughts had become. The sound echoed throughout her body, making it nearly impossible for her to speak. She simply nodded her head in response.

It had to be the music, the alcohol and the unaccustomed closeness making her feel so lightheaded. Cade was just a familiar body in a strange environment. Or maybe this wild rush of excitement could be chalked up to too many years of self-imposed celibacy. Maybe she should make more of an effort to improve her social life.

Whatever the case, she immediately withdrew from Cade's embrace when the song ended. Then she mentally chastised herself for feeling chilled and bereft.

"I think I'd better visit the restroom," she mumbled, feeling his curious gaze on her, but refusing to look him in the eyes.

He cleared his throat. "I guess it's time for me to go hang around the men's room, too."

The band started another number, this one livelier, and everyone on the dance floor began to shift into lines. She and Cade dodged bodies until they were near the restroom doors.

"I'll just be a minute," she managed before ducking into the relative safety of the ladies' room. There were several other women using the facilities, but she paid them no attention.

Expelling a deep, pained breath, she dared a glance at the mirror above the sink. Her pupils were wide, her face flushed, her expression distant and dreamy. She swiftly composed her features. She had to get a grip.

It helped to splash cool water on her face. After another few minutes, her heart had stopped racing and her nerves were nearly back to normal. This had to stop. She couldn't keep coming apart in his arms. He might be interested in a willing body, but she didn't indulge in casual sex. However much their bodies might yearn for intimacy, she couldn't risk it.

From here on out she'd ignore the sexual tension and keep a discreet distance between them. She would not allow a fleeting attraction to destroy their working relationship. Nor would she let him con her into another date like tonight. She'd refuse to accompany him anywhere outside the office. He could do his sleuthing without her.

While Sallie mentally lectured herself, she patted her face dry and then ran cool water over her wrists. After smoothing her hair and checking her reflection again, she decided it was safe to rejoin Cade.

Her gaze fell on him as soon as she stepped out the door. He was looking in the opposite direction, down a darkened hallway toward an exit sign. Sallie caught sight of a short, thin little man who was warily watching them. When she took a step closer, the other man bolted out the door.

Cade glanced her way. "Stay here, I'll be right back," he ordered before taking off in pursuit of their mystery man. Sallie didn't even hesitate. No way was she staying in this place alone. She was hot on his heels as he left the building.

The alley behind the tavern was narrow and littered with trash. The lighting was dim, casting weird shadows, but it was easy to see that the little man was headed around the building toward the parking lot. Cade was a few yards behind him, and Sallie followed, but more cautiously.

By the time she'd rounded the building, an engine had roared to life and a dark-colored compact car was reversing out of a parking spot. Sallie saw Cade climbing into a company pickup truck and ran in his direction.

He'd thrown the gears into reverse by the time she neared. He shoved open the passenger door to let her in.

"I thought I told you to stay put!" he shouted.

"I don't have to take orders on the weekend," she tossed back at him, breathing roughly after her sprint. She climbed into the truck, slammed the door and turned toward him. "You're not leaving me alone in that place!"

"Fasten your seat belt," he said while swinging the pickup out of the parking lot onto a two-way street.

"Yours isn't fastened," she reminded sharply, reaching for her belt.

"I'm in a hurry."

"All the more reason."

He didn't argue, but pulled his belt around with one hand and concentrated on the taillights of the car rapidly putting distance between them.

"How'd he get so far ahead of us?" she wanted to know.

"Someone was waiting for him."

Cade's tone was grim, and Sallie understood his frustration. It appeared they were dealing with two mystery men instead of one. Not a good development.

"Why do you suppose he ran?"

"He was coming toward me until he caught sight of you. Maybe seeing two company execs spooked him."

"You think he recognized me?"

"Must have."

"I didn't recognize him, did you?"

"I've never seen him, but that doesn't mean he's not an employee," he said as he took a corner with tires squealing.

The truck rocked back and forth, and Sallie braced herself with both hands on the dash. They were gaining on the compact, but the driver was running traffic lights and stop signs. Fortunately, the streets were almost deserted and there were no pedestrians. Cade was barely slowing for intersections, either.

"What are you planning to do if we actually catch up with these guys?" she asked, her body swaying sideways as they made another sharp turn.

"I just want to get close enough to read the license plate. That'll give us something concrete to work with."

She kept her gaze glued to the car ahead of them. It fishtailed around another corner, and then sped up again.

They were still more than a city block behind it when the flash of brake lights signaled it was slowing for a turn. They'd nearly reduced the distance between them when the car made a sharp left into a narrow alley.

Cade swore softly and immediately slowed the truck. In another few seconds they were approaching the same alley, but he didn't make the turn.

"We're going to lose them!" Sallie insisted, "They went down the alley!"

"I know, but we're not," he said, his tone grim.

"What?" she demanded, disbelieving. "I thought you wanted to get a license number!"

"I do, but it's too risky to follow them down an unfamiliar alley. It could be a trap."

"How can it be a trap? They didn't know we'd be following them!" she argued, twisting in the seat to look behind them and impatient for him to turn back.

"I'm not taking any chances with you along."

"What?" This time Sallie's response was irate as she turned her attention more fully to him. "You mean you'd follow them if you were alone?"

"Damn straight," he growled in disgust.

"I can't believe it!" she shouted, grabbing his forearm and shaking him urgently. "How can you just let them get away? They might know who's at the bottom of all our problems."

His jaw had locked into a hard line that she privately thought of as his bullish expression. That meant he wouldn't be badgered into changing his mind, and that made her angrier.

"I don't want you protecting me at the cost of the company. I want to go back there and see who these thugs are!"

Cade had circled the block and was nearing the alley again, but he made no attempt to turn. The truck slowed and they both peered down the dark passageway, but no vehicle could be seen.

"Damn!" Sallie hissed a rare cuss word in her frustration. She'd actually been enjoying their chase. Her adrenaline was high, and she wasn't happy about being cheated out of some modicum of success.

Cade shot her a quick glance. "We'll find out who they are. It'll just take a little more time."

"It wouldn't have to take more time if you'd have followed them," she grumbled.

"A license number isn't worth the risk. Even if we got them cornered, there's nothing we could have done. For all we know they're armed and dangerous."

Sallie hadn't considered that angle. She sat back in the seat, heaved a big sigh, and shoved her hair behind her ears. She didn't know what they could have done, she only knew she was thoroughly annoyed at not having the chance to do anything.

What annoyed her most was that Cade had stifled his impulse to follow the car because of her. The last thing she wanted or needed in life was to be protected by another well-meaning man who thought he knew how best to keep her safe.

"There's a chance he wanted to talk to you, but was afraid to do it out in the open. Maybe if we'd have followed him, he would have stopped the car and talked," she argued.

"Not likely," said Cade. "I'd have to be a real idiot to involve you in a meeting like that. I was crazy enough to chase them with you in the truck."

She fumed at the idea. "I'm not a hot-house flower, you know. I'm perfectly capable of thinking for myself. When given the choice between a sleazy bar and a high-speed chase, I'd always choose the chase!"

"Speaking of sleazy bars," Cade said, his tone lighter. "We skipped out without paying the check. They're liable to sic their thugs on us."

Sallie was still too angry to see the humor. She was ready to thump him herself. She'd never been so excited, felt so alive and adventurous. Then, in a matter of seconds, he'd slapped her with disappointment. All for the sake of protecting her. She looked straight ahead and crossed her arms over her chest, her body language eloquent with displeasure.

They drove a few miles in silence before Cade spoke again. This time his voice rippled with amusement.

"Are you pouting?"

She didn't answer, nor acknowledge the question. She was royally ticked. They'd kept their relationship strictly professional for five years with no problems. In less than twenty-four hours of getting more personal, he'd incited her to wrath twice already. She liked her calm, comfortable life, yet he seemed to be pushing all her buttons and destroying her peace of mind.

"Hell, I think you're giving me the silent treatment," said Cade in amazement. "You've never done that before."

"I've never been so angry with you before!" she snapped.

In response, he laughed, the low, husky sound echoing in the cab of the truck. It should have annoyed her, but instead, it sent a frisson of sensual pleasure skittering along her nerves. And that annoyed her. She continued to glare at him until he'd stopped chuckling.

"You're going to get us both killed if you don't watch where you're driving." Her tone held a bite, but it was hard to stay angry with a man whose deep, sexy laughter sent a thrill of excitement dancing through adrenaline-pumped blood.

Cade shook his head as his chuckles gradually died. He pulled into the Tumbleweed Tavern's parking lot. Nothing had changed in the time they'd been gone.

Cade's Challenge

"Would you like to come inside or would you rather stay locked in the truck?" he asked with exaggerated politeness.

"Now you ask," she groused, but some of her good humor had returned. "Why are men unfailingly polite when it doesn't matter?"

"I'm not gonna touch that question," he replied, stopping the truck at the entrance. He opened his door and stepped down to the pavement. As he turned to her, his irresistible grin was briefly illuminated.

Sallie tried not to be charmed. "Don't forget to leave the waitress a tip," she commanded.

"Yes, ma'am."

He clicked the lock, slammed the door, and strode into the building, leaving her to watch his retreating figure.

Her memory conjured the hard warmth of his body pressed against hers and her own body's reactions. Every little nerve ending tingled at the memory of his big, gentle hands on her back, his breath teasing her ear.

"Stop it!" she admonished herself aloud. She did not want to think of him in a sexual manner. They'd worked together too long and too hard to throw it all away now. She'd just have to rein in her silly imaginings.

And she had to get a grip on her temper. It had raged out of control in her teen years, but she'd matured and learned to redirect the passionate side of her nature. At least, she thought she had, until last night.

Cade returned in less than ten minutes, and she leaned over to open the door for him.

"All set," he told her, climbing behind the wheel again. "We were forgiven when I paid twice what we owed and included a hefty tip. Money talks at the Tumbleweed Tavern."

"Yes, I'm sure it does," she agreed. Her parents had raised her with that adage, and they'd rarely been proven wrong. "You didn't happen to ask if anyone saw our mystery man or if anyone could identify him?"

Cade hesitated just long enough for her to realize he didn't want to tell her.

"You did find out something, didn't you?" she asked, carefully containing her excitement at the thought.

"I described him to the bartender, and he thinks he might have seen him around."

She waited for him to expand, but he didn't offer any other information. "That's it? That's all you're going to tell me?" she asked. "You're planning to take me home and then go look for him, aren't you?"

Cade's brow knitted in a frown, and she knew she was right.

"I'm going to take you home and have Steven meet me there," he explained, reaching for his mobile phone. He punched in Steven's pager number. "Maybe the two of us can get to the bottom of this thing."

Sallie didn't comment. She was feeling strangely put out by his attitude, yet she couldn't understand her own reaction. It made sense for Cade and Steven to work on solving their problems. Normally, she was perfectly happy to let them handle security while she took care of business.

Tonight, she resented being excluded. The feelings of resentment were even more troubling because she rarely got so excited that she would feel this kind of disappointment. She kept her expectations low so that she didn't have regrets.

Both of them were quiet as they made the trip to her house. The parking lot in front of the condo was well lit. Cade pulled the truck into a slot near her car. Steven returned his call and they decided to meet back at the tavern.

"Don't bother to get out," Sallie said when he closed the phone and shut off the truck's engine. "Thanks for dinner and the ride home. Good night," she added and jumped from the cab.

After slamming the door shut, she headed toward her porch without a backward glance. Her anger had returned for some inexplicable reason that even she didn't understand.

The sound of his door slamming made her tenser. She wasn't surprised that he intended to see her safely to the door, but her annoyance increased with his thoughtfulness. Her emotions were in such turmoil that she needed some time alone to sort them all out.

Cade called to her as she slipped the key in the lock and punched numbers on the new code pad.

"Sallie, wait!"

75

She stiffened and reluctantly turned to face him as he came up the sidewalk.

"Let me take a quick look around your house."

She wanted to refuse, yet knew it would be stupid. Pushing the door open, she waved him inside, but didn't follow. She didn't want to see him roaming through her house again. Didn't want to feel his presence the rest of the night. Instead, she waited impatiently on the front porch.

In a few minutes, he returned, assuring her that the house was empty and safe.

"Thank you," she said, trying, but failing to infuse any warmth into her words.

He stared at her for a few long minutes, the air between them throbbing with tension.

"Are you okay?" he finally asked.

"I'm fine. Thanks for an interesting evening. You can go find Steven now."

For another long minute, they continued to stare at each other with neither moving nor seeming to breathe.

Finally, Cade broke the tense silence. "You're angry again."

She was so angry she was quivering with it. It was a silly, emotional reaction that was totally out of character. That's what made it all the more intense and alarming.

Her parents had been excessively protective. After a love affair gone horribly wrong, she'd been content with her mundane lifestyle. But for a few minutes, she'd experienced an adrenaline high, the thrill of an unexpected adventure and a shared camaraderie. She'd liked it a lot. Then he'd squashed the euphoria to ensure her safety.

When she didn't reply, Cade reached a hand out, touching her arm. Sallie reacted as if he'd hit her, and quickly jerked her arm out of reach.

She knew it was a mistake as soon as she made the involuntary defensive move. Cade's whole body tensed. Then one arm shot out to circle her waist and drag her intimately close. He used the other to cup the back of her head and tug her face close enough that she could feel his breath on her lips.

"Don't." Her weak whisper was smothered by hard, demanding lips. His mouth crushed hers with insistent pressure. For a brief instant, Sallie was too startled to respond. Her lips were locked, her body stiff and unresponsive.

Then he made a low, urgent sound in his throat that was hungry and coaxing and totally arousing. It did funny things to her insides, and some of the stiffness went out of her muscles.

Ever so slowly, as if in a trance, she molded her lips to the shape of his, parting them just enough to invite a deepening of the kiss. Accompanied by a deep-throated groan, the invasion and exploration by his warm, wet tongue made her head swim and her blood flow hot in her veins.

She clutched his arms to steady herself even though she was at no risk of falling. Then her hands slid to his chest, her fingers curling and uncurling, like the flexing of a cat's claws against the rock-solid wall of muscle.

Cade's arm around her waist tightened, drawing her closer while his hand tilted her head so he could thrust his tongue deeper into her mouth. Sallie heard a low, strangled sound of need, and belatedly realized it came from her own throat.

She allowed her tongue to duel with his for a few long minutes and then sucked it so greedily that his whole body bucked in response. His hands slid down her back to cup her bottom, lifting her on her toes to rock the rigid evidence of his desire against the cradle of her thighs.

The hard strength of his arousal burned through the layers of clothes, inflaming her even more. Suddenly, there wasn't enough air in her lungs. Her pulse pounded riotously. A deep, aching throb began low in her belly, sending a hot current of electricity throughout the rest of her body. Her skin sizzled and her toes curled.

This couldn't be happening to her, she mentally argued as she fell more deeply under his sensually drugging spell. What was wrong with her? Cade's kisses made her feel dizzy and light-headed and hungry for more.

It had to be the alcohol in her system, she thought, as frantic for an explanation as she was for his next kiss. It had to be the beer. She'd had some sort of strange reaction to it or she wouldn't be feeling so wild and wanton and out of control.

"Cade!" she cried out in panic the next time their mouths parted for air. "I don't want this!"

As abruptly as he'd grabbed her, he released her. They both struggled for balance, gulping for breath as tension pulsed between them. Trembling from head to toe, Sallie quickly turned and entered the house.

"Lock your doors," Cade's harsh command followed her. "All of them!"

ഗ്ഗ

Hidden in the late night shadows, he watched, his body shaking with fury. Langden had crossed the line! He couldn't condemn the man for wanting his sweet Sallie, but that didn't give him the right to touch her.

She belonged to him. He'd been watching over her for years now. Once she'd grown into a mature woman, he'd known they were meant to be together. He'd made meticulous plans for their future. She deserved the best, and he intended to give it to her.

He'd recognized Langden's growing interest in Sallie. That's why he'd had Winerman get a part-time job at the plant to cause a little trouble and keep tabs on the management. Langden needed a warning. He needed to focus on running the damned company and stay away from Sallie. But the plan had backfired when that wimp He planned to put Winerman out of the picture for good. It wouldn't happen again, he thought smugly. Winerman was out of the picture for good.

    Now he had to get Sallie away from Langden or get Langden out of the picture, too. He hadn't decided which would be best at this point. He'd give it more thought. He always gave all his decisions careful thought.

Chapter Five

Cade prowled his office like a caged tiger, pacing back and forth, back and forth. He raked his hands through his hair in frustration while he tried to deal with the latest blow to his peace of mind.

Sallie. She had him tied in knots.

The way she'd moved with him and against him while they danced—like ice melting into molten lava and overheating his senses. She'd slowly lost her stiffness, going warm and pliant, and he'd nearly lost control.

Just the thought of the kiss they'd shared made his gut tighten and fire sizzle through his veins. The explosive desire had shaken him badly. Now he went hard and hot every time he thought about holding her in his arms. The memories had kept him edgy and restless all weekend.

Until his brother had married, he'd never given much thought to settling down with one woman. Over the past year, the urge for a mate and his own family had grown stronger and stronger. He knew a lot of women who wanted marriage and a few who only wanted an occasional lover. He had no idea where Sallie fit into the equation, or if she fit at all, yet his feelings for her kept getting more and more complicated.

He'd come to work early to get a grip, but thoughts of her were even stronger here. She'd decorated the whole place with his preferences in mind. Everything from the sturdy, practical furnishings to the southwestern landscapes suited him to a T.

She'd created a perfect setting for him, one that had always been conducive to clear thinking. Now all he could think about was her and the influence she'd had on him these past few years. How well she knew him and how little he knew her. How their chemistry had taken on a life of its own.

Cade hadn't thought their relationship could get any more complicated. Then Steven had given him the security report.

"While I was running a security check on personnel, I ran Sallie's name through my sources, too," he'd said.

"What the hell? When I said everybody, I didn't mean to include her." She'd become more of a partner than an assistant. He considered her an invaluable member of their team. She had keen business and people instincts, plus she kept him focused. He trusted her implicitly.

"I figured as much, but it started with just a random check of her social security number."

"She won't be too pleased if she finds out you've been prying into her private life."

"That's just it. I didn't pry, because I kept running into brick walls every time I tried to access personal information. She has bank accounts, a driver's license, and a library card," Steven had insisted. "But nothing that dates back farther than five years ago when she started to work for you. It's as if she didn't exist before then. Or, she didn't exist under the name Sallie Archer."

Cade didn't like any of the possible scenarios for that kind of security. He didn't have any reason to doubt Sallie's loyalty, but his curiosity had been piqued.

"Have you ever run into anything like this before?"

"Sure, but the options are limited. The FBI's witness protection program was my first thought, yet even those files can be accessed if the hacker's good enough. Some of my contacts are that good."

Cade didn't want to know the details, especially if they involved questionable methods. "And your sources couldn't find anything on Sallie?"

"Nothing."

"I've always thought she had a wealthy upbringing. Could she completely change her identity if she had enough money or the right connections?"

"It's possible, but that kind of money and influence usually leaves a trail."

"If she's part of the witness protection system, that intruder would have had her changing identities again." The thought that she could disappear without a trace chilled him to the bone.

"She's not stupid," said Steven. "And she acted more annoyed than scared."

"Maybe that was an act. Maybe she's scared out of her mind, but doesn't want us to know." He didn't like that idea at all. "What are some of the other options? How and why could she have her past wiped clean? Could she be hiding from someone? An abusive ex-husband, a stalker?"

"In that case, she might be able to change her identity, but she wouldn't be able to change her social security number or totally wipe out her past. Not legally, at least."

"Maybe she got into trouble as a kid. Got involved with a bad crowd as a teen. With enough money and clout, you could probably pay to bury your past."

"Maybe." Steven hadn't been convinced. "But I checked every listing on her original application form and kept coming up blank. I couldn't validate one reference for birth records, past employers or educational background. Nothing clicked. The way I see it, everything on that form was falsified."

Sallie had deliberately lied and deceived him from the very beginning? "Why? Why the hell would she do that?"

"I don't know. My suggestion would be to ask her and see what she says. It's been five years since she supplied the information."

"Does Sallie strike you as conniving or dishonest?"

Steven shook his head slowly. "I would have sworn she's as straight and trustworthy as they come, but maybe she had an ulterior motive for hiring on with you."

"I trust her implicitly. Always have. When she came to work for me all I had was a patent and a plan. That's not the stuff of corporate espionage."

"Doesn't make sense," Steven agreed. "Did anyone try to pressure you into selling your engine patent? Offer you partnerships that you refused? Did you tick off anyone important in the industry?"

"I had lots of offers, but none more persistent than the others." He shook his head, his frown deepening. "I can't see Sallie as a corporate spy."

"Doesn't add up," agreed Steven.

"So, how can her secrets have anything to do with our current problems?"

"Someone from her past might be trying to blackmail or threaten her."

Cade's hands clenched into fists and his temper spiked. Did her secrets have anything to do with the company's recent problems? If so, why hadn't she warned him? What else was she hiding? He'd always trusted her. How could she betray that trust?

Then he remembered the car chase Friday night. "I don't think she's afraid of anyone or anything from her past. She got really ticked when I wouldn't follow that car down the alley. She wanted to catch it."

"Or lead you into a trap."

The room went quiet at Steven's bald suggestion. Cade couldn't believe that of Sallie. As chief of security, maybe Steven had to consider all the options, but he had to trust his own instincts where she was concerned.

They'd known each other too long for him to suspect her of that sort of treachery. He'd have bet the business that she couldn't be bribed or coerced into doing anything illegal or even unethical. But that was before he'd learned about her original deception. Everything she'd put on her application was a lie. Everything he assumed about her past was a lie.

That stung, and he was still smarting hours later, still trying to sort out the tangle of emotions. Hurt. Anger. Frustration. What he hated most was the hurting. She was coming to mean a whole lot more to him than a colleague. The feelings were deeper, stronger, more complex and hard to define.

Tangled with the emotions was a relentless physical desire that kept humming through his body. Every thought of Sallie triggered a throbbing need in him. She'd become a problem on several levels. He hadn't seen her yet today, even though he was well aware of her presence in the outer office. Cade steeled himself for the inevitable confrontation, and then hit the intercom button.

"Sallie, would you please ask the receptionist to hold our calls and come in here for a few minutes?"

At her agreement, he started to take a seat behind his desk, and then changed his mind. He didn't want that much space between them, so he perched on the edge of his desk and waited.

She came through the door and quietly closed it behind her. So slim and elegant and cool with her neatly secured hair and her aloof manner. She'd shed her suit jacket and was wearing only a sleeveless white blouse with a soft, flowing skirt. It suited her trim body and graceful curves.

The sight of her made his mouth go dry, his muscles tighten and his heart hammer. Their date Friday night had forever changed his opinion of her. Once he'd felt her melting in his arms, he'd been lost.

God, he had it bad. The hunger for her fed off itself, growing and gnawing at him. He'd known more than his fair share of women. Several of them had frustrated him, challenged him, and thrilled him. The conflicting emotions he felt for Sallie made all the others pale in significance.

He subdued his libido and motioned for her to have a seat, his gaze never leaving her features. Even though she was an expert at concealing her emotions, he noted a brief spurt of panic in her eyes before she hid them with her lashes.

What panicked her most? Did she have an inkling of what Steven had discovered or was the panic purely feminine? Did she think their working relationship was on the line? Or was she afraid he might overstep the bounds of employer? Make demands she couldn't or wouldn't accept? Did she think him despicable for acting on their attraction? He'd been a little rough, but she'd been just as involved in that kiss as he'd been.

Cade waited until she sat down and lifted her gaze to him again before speaking. "Steven gave me a rundown of his background check of personnel."

Sallie nodded, her expression subtly changing from wary to curious. Apparently, she felt they were on safe ground, which meant her wariness had stemmed from personal, not professional concerns.

"He found something interesting?" she asked.

"Not much in regard to our company problems, but he reported some interesting facts about your background."

She tensed again, her eyes going wide with surprise. And alarm? Her posture stiffened. "You ordered a background check on me?"

"I didn't order it. I just told Steven to check everyone, and he included you."

Her eyes sparkled with indignation. That, in itself, was evidence of the change in their relationship. Until last week, she rarely let him see past her detached professionalism.

"Why? What did he expect to find? A criminal record? Outstanding warrants?"

"He just followed my orders. I told him to run a complete check on personnel and you are part of the staff," he reminded tersely. "He did a basic check on your original application and got more curious with every dead end. The more he delved, the more inconsistencies he found."

"All that information is years old!" she insisted, her tone heated. "What possible difference could it make now?"

"The difference is in a little matter called trust. And there's the matter of me hiring you in good faith. You're still an employee on my staff, and I expect better of you."

Cade watched her cheeks flare with color and felt an answering heat in his loins, despite his frustration with the situation. He enjoyed ruffling her composure. It turned him on to see her shed the cool indifference and get riled. Since she was playing hell with his composure, he didn't feel any remorse at returning the favor. He wanted nothing but open, honest emotion between them.

"As for the investigation, it makes no difference." He was proud of the calm in his own voice. "What really matters is that you've lied to me since day one. I'd like an explanation."

The sudden pallor in her cheeks and stricken look in her eyes alarmed him. His arms were crossed over his chest, and he clenched his hands into fists to keep from reaching for her. He couldn't back down now. He had to know where they stood, both personally and professionally.

Sallie rose from the chair and faced him, eye-to-eye. There was a fine tremor in her voice when she started to speak, but she cleared her throat.

"I'll type up my resignation this afternoon and start looking for a replacement."

Alarm propelled Cade to action. He slid to his feet as she turned from him, and quickly grabbed her arm. Heat flashed through him when his fingers touched soft, bare skin.

"I don't want your resignation. I want an explanation," he insisted irritably.

"There's nothing to explain. I was young and desperate for work, so I lied about my age and background. I knew it was wrong and that it could backfire someday. I also knew if I'd told you the truth, you wouldn't have considered me for the job."

"You're so sure of that?" Her attitude had him growling. "So test me. What is the truth? Why did you reinvent yourself?"

Sallie tugged her arm from his grasp and leveled a fierce frown at him. "I was only twenty at the time, so I lied. I knew you'd be more comfortable working with someone your own age."

"Twenty?" That caught him off guard. He couldn't believe she'd barely been out of high school. Even five years ago she'd been more poised and sophisticated than all the other job applicants.

"You mean you're only twenty-five now? I thought you were nearly that old when I hired you."

"My point, exactly. You wouldn't have given me a chance to prove myself. You'd have dismissed me for being too young."

"If you were twenty, does that mean you lied about your schooling, too? You didn't have any formal business training?" She couldn't have acquired her incredible skills by accident, nor could anyone be born with so much business savvy.

"I was an overachiever," she explained derisively. "I finished high school at sixteen and college at nineteen. I didn't lie about my qualifications, only the specifics of my schooling. I have a business degree."

Cade's tone and expression were grim. He didn't like being duped any more than the next guy.

"So, your lies were selective. That's encouraging," he grumbled. "What about your name and personal background? How did you rationalize all the years of dishonesty? Even the name's phony."

That gave her pause. She shifted her gaze from his and hedged. "It's not fake. Sallie Archer is my legal name."

"Just not the one you were given at birth, right?" He hated it when she refused to look him in the eyes. "What's wrong with your given name? Is there some stigma attached? Some reason you felt the need to hide the truth? Bury your past?"

"I haven't done anything to be ashamed of, if that's what you're asking. Or anything illegal. I just didn't want to be judged by my family name without any thought as to my personal qualifications and professional skills."

"That's assuming your family name is well-known enough to influence my judgment. Who are you? The daughter of some Hollywood celebrity? A politician's princess? The innocent child of a Mafia boss or a serial killer?"

Sallie's gaze snapped back to his, the frost in her eyes a direct contrast to her features flushed with temper. When she responded, her voice dripped ice.

"My father is Carlton Harriman, the third."

A long minute of utter silence followed her announcement.

Cade continued to stare at her, trying to curb his stunned reaction. Harriman wasn't exactly a household name, but he was an icon in the business world. Her father was one of the wealthiest men alive, barring oil sheiks, and he probably owned some prime real estate with an oil well or two, as well.

Hotels, casinos, waterfront properties in all the finest locations. Harriman owned whole islands, and was reputed to be one of the shrewdest developers who ever lived. To call him rich and influential was like calling a mountain lion a kitty cat.

Suddenly, all the pieces fit. It was easy to understand why Sallie had excelled at everything—the maturity, sophistication and business acumen.

"That little bit of my personal history always has the same effect," she complained, irritation apparent in her tone and in the rigid lines of her body. "It strikes people speechless. Just imagine how you would have reacted had I told you that from the start. Then imagine how difficult it was for me to find work."

Cade recovered his composure, but fought a smile. He loved seeing her rattled. It made her seem as vulnerable and needy as the rest of humankind.

"Poor little rich girl?" he taunted.

It drew the anticipated response. Sallie turned more fully toward him. Her chin rose, and anger flared in her eyes. He'd definitely hit a nerve. She bristled, but he wanted more. The hell with her parentage, he wanted to shatter years of cultured control. He wanted her to rant and rave and lash out at him like she had last week.

Then he wanted all that wildness funneled into passion.

Desire razored through him, hot and primitive. He wanted her to help unleash it. She'd taken his emotions on a roller coaster ride, and he wanted to do the same to her.

"So you think I should feel sorry for you and just forget that you're a consummate liar?" he jeered softly.

That struck a chord, and she struck out at him. He caught her right hand when it swung toward his face, then the left when it followed. Just that basic a physical contact sent a shudder through him. He held her wrists tightly as they glared at each other for a few tense, shocked seconds. Tension was a wild thing, making the air around them sizzle.

Then he slowly, steadily drew her hands around his neck and hauled her against his chest, slamming his mouth onto hers with tightly leashed impatience. He'd been starving for the taste of her, craving her mouth like a marathoner craved water.

Her lips remained obstinately tight, her body rigid as she strained backward to avoid his kiss. Cade mentally cursed his lack of restraint, and eased the pressure on her mouth. He loosened his iron grip on her arms, and then used his lips and tongue to soothe her in gentle apology.

"Sallie, Sallie, Sallie," he whispered. "You're driving me crazy." The husky admission vibrated with emotion, and drained some of the stiffness from her body.

Somewhere in the middle of the next long, coaxing kiss, she stopped straining for distance between them and began to relax a little more. Her mouth parted ever so slowly and sweetly, gradually welcoming the invasion of his tongue. Taking full advantage, he swept it across her teeth, into the hollows of her cheeks and then along the length of her tongue. She tasted as sweet as he remembered.

He loosened his grip on her wrists, but she didn't retreat. She shifted closer and locked her arms around his neck, freeing him to caress the length of her bare arms, from wrist to elbow to shoulders. Her skin was so soft, so smooth, so supple. He wanted to explore every inch of her. Taste every delectable centimeter.

Their mouths parted on breathless sighs, and he busied himself planting kisses along the curve of her jaw. He massaged some of the tension from her shoulders, and then buried his fingers in her hair. Her neck enticed him next with its softness and the subtle sweetness of her perfume. He sucked the pulse beating erratically at her throat, and then trapped her tiny moan with deeper, more searching kisses.

Tunneling his fingers into her hair, he slowly worked it loose until he could gather the satiny tresses in both his hands. Eyes closed, her lashes were feathered over pale cheeks, her expression dreamy. It made him ache just to look at her. He used his grip on her to tilt her head, allowing their mouths to lock more completely. Their tongues mated in perfect harmony.

The kisses were hot and heady, making him dizzy. He kept going back for another and another and another. She returned them with a fervor that set him on fire.

Cade grew more aroused and restless by the second. Blood sang through his veins in a riotous rhythm, making him hotter and harder with each beat of his heart. He couldn't get enough of her, her taste, her scent, her feel. He wanted to gobble her up, feel her against him skin-to-skin, and join their bodies in the most elemental fashion.

When next they gasped for breath, he scoured her face with kisses, brushing her nose, caressing her eyes, and skimming the softness of her cheeks before he homed in on her mouth again. This time, she greedily sucked his tongue into her mouth, and he felt the pull of desire deep in his gut.

His fingers slid to her neck, kneading and encouraging. Then they drifted down her spine to its base, where they rubbed a little longer. Suddenly urgent for the feel of more skin, he tugged her blouse from the waistband of her skirt and slipped his hands beneath the fabric. She felt warm and soft and sweetly feminine. He took his time to enjoy the sensual pleasure.

Sallie rocked against him, gripping him more tightly, and he tugged her closer. Shifting until his back was against the wall, he spread his legs, urging her into the cradle of his thighs. When she pressed herself against him, he nearly came undone. She fit perfectly, chest-to-chest and hip-to-hip. A shudder racked him when she snuggled herself against the hard ridge of flesh straining his jeans.

A moan of pleasure erupted from deep in his throat. When their mouths parted, he nudged her sideways so that he could slide his lips down her throat to her chest. He eased the neck of her blouse aside to scatter kisses across her breastbone and the gentle swell of her breasts. Her sexy moan was little more than a whisper of warm breath against his ear, but he felt it to the tips of his toes.

His hands moved to her hips, his fingers involuntarily flexing into her tight flesh. He urged her still closer, shuddering violently when she rocked against him in feminine demand. Desire, hot and raw, clawed at his insides, making his blood thicken and his legs tremble. His mouth sought hers again for another hot, wet kiss until he got dangerously close to losing control and embarrassing himself. So close, that he dragged his mouth from hers and sucked in air, fighting for calm. He needed a few seconds to get a grip and clear his head.

Instead, he got seduced by the feel of her lips at his neck. Tentative at first with the wet flick of her tongue, her caress grew bolder until she was sucking the pulse that pounded erratically at his throat. He felt the pull deep in his groin, and his knees grew weak.

His grunt of pleasure started low in his belly and surged slowly up toward the muscles of his throat. The same muscles she alternately bathed and sucked. She made him so hot that he knew he had to concentrate on her, on the feel of her, not on what she was doing to him. With that thought in mind, he buried his face in the opening of her blouse.

The first few buttons gave way with little effort, exposing a lacy camisole. Cade found her pouting nipples through the silky fabric and gave them the same attention she'd just given his neck. He licked each one, slowly and lavishly, rotating his tongue back and forth until they were hard and tight. She pleased him with a mewing sound of pleasure.

Then his hunger got the best of him, and he burrowed his face under the fabric to the sweetest, softest skin. He slid a hand to one breast and caressed the nipple with his thumb while taking the other deeply into his mouth. He sucked greedily, using his whole mouth to caress the hard, plump tip.

The sound of Sallie's shuddering breaths made him hotter, harder and even needier. He savored the sound and feel of her until she started rocking herself against the hardness of his arousal. Her body implored him in age-old feminine demand, and he struggled for control again.

So good. It felt so damn good.

He slid his hands under her skirt, shoving it up and out of the way until he could grasp her buttocks. The tight flex of silk-covered muscle had his blood blazing like wildfire. Hunger roared through him.

Her movements grew more agitated, and he rubbed himself against her as hard as clothing restraints would allow. She arched into him, making him almost lightheaded with desire. He sucked her nipple more deeply into his mouth, clutched her still closer, and began to grind himself against her.

She whimpered, and he almost lost it.

So responsive.

So impossibly sweet and sexy.

He sucked harder and pulled her tighter, straining to give her the contact she needed. Her hands clutched at his hair. She bit his neck, and he quaked with the pleasure of it. Suddenly desperate for the taste of her, he found her mouth again. His tongue plundered in a primitive mating ritual.

He felt the heat of her through the denim of his jeans. It had him gasping for air, clutching her even tighter, and grinding himself against her with all his strength. He was precariously close to exploding when her muffled cry echoed in his ear. Her body convulsed against him, and she shuddered with release.

She came apart in his arms, and it took a lifetime of discipline to keep from doing the same. The throbbing in his loins bordered on agony, stunning him. Hot, harsh breaths burned his lungs as he fought for air and restraint. He didn't want to settle for quickie sex in his office.

He'd never come so close to losing it. His legs shook, his body quaking right along with hers.

So much passion.

Incredible. She had an incredible affect on him. He burned for her. With very little effort, she'd set him on fire.

He was in serious trouble here.

"You are so hot and so sexy," he whispered in ragged voice. "You make me weak."

He wrapped her in his arms, rocking her gently, just holding her until the tremors stopped shivering through them. Her breath was hot against his neck, her nipples jabbed at his chest. He forced himself to focus on everything but his unsatisfied desire. He had to pull himself together.

They'd just shot their professional relationship to hell. He'd never be able to look at her again without remembering how fantastic she made him feel. Or how exquisitely responsive she could be.

They'd passed the point of no return.

It didn't bother him, but he didn't know what to expect from Sallie. She was such a stickler for professionalism.

Her grip on his neck loosened. She eased more space between their bodies, and Cade felt a pang of regret. He wanted more time. He didn't want to lose the heat or closeness yet. She'd just given him one of the most extraordinary experiences in his life, and he didn't want to let her go.

When she finally pulled free of his arms, she didn't look at him. The first twinge of concern registered. Then she turned her back to him and slowly straightened her clothes.

His heart stuttered when she tried to speak and had to clear the huskiness from her voice. Damn he wanted her. But it was more than physical, more even than a passionate hunger for her body. He wanted to know her without inhibitions. Without the worry of professional ethics. He wanted so much more.

If her spine hadn't been rigid, her chin so high, he'd have reached for her again. He waited, tense and troubled, for her reaction to what they'd just shared. When it came, it nearly blew him away.

"I hope you're satisfied with that bit of revenge. I'm resigning as of this minute. You can keep my severance pay in lieu of a two-week notice."

"What the hell? Sallie, wait!" Her stiff, wounded look stunned him. He started after her, but she slammed the door in his face. The sound echoed in his head like a drum.

His legs were still shaky. They folded, and he slid to the floor with a thud. Then he banged his head back against the wall in frustration. The resounding thump echoed around the emptiness of the office.

Rubbing his hands down his face, he wondered how she'd managed to misinterpret his intentions. There hadn't been a thought of vengeance in his mind. No thought to punish her. Just need—urgent, life-altering need. How could she take something so sweet and twist it so badly?

He lost track of time as he sat there and tried to pull himself together. A knock on the door finally had him heaving himself to his feet just as Steven strode into the room. His security chief looked tense and annoyed.

Join the club.

"Hell, Cade. I came in here to drill you about upsetting Sallie, but you look as bad as she does."

"Yeah." He raked a hand through his hair. "She quit."

Steven wisely didn't ask for details. "You're not going to let her go, are you?"

"Has she left the building already?"

"I passed her downstairs in the lobby. She was on her way out."

"I'm going after her. Will you have the receptionist clear our appointments for the rest of the day and lock this place up?"

"Sure."

"Thanks."

"Good luck."

Cade figured he was going to need a whole lot more than luck to make this right.

ಬಂಬಂಜ

He followed his sweet Sallie when she left work in the middle of the day, looking more distressed than he'd seen her look in years. Langden had to be responsible and he'd have to answer for that.

They thought they'd defeated him with their high-tech security, but there were other ways to get her attention. He just didn't like changing plans and taking action without enough time to work out all the details.

Chapter Six

As soon as Sallie got home, she stripped off her clothes, right down to her still-damp undergarments, and stuffed them in the hamper. Heat raced through her each time she thought of Cade's mouth on her body. All her senses were on overload, and she couldn't seem to squelch the erotic sensations. Every thought, every action, every move she made reminded her of the disaster in his office.

She took a quick, cool shower, hoping to calm her riotous pulse. The deep-breathing exercises she'd done in the car hadn't helped much. After drying briskly, she pulled on fresh panties and a pair of blue silk shorts. She'd just slipped the matching tank top over her head when she heard the doorbell.

Mumbling all the way to the door, hoping to find a salesman or paperboy on the other side, she peered through the peephole. Her mouth went dry, her recently cooled flesh overheating at the sight of Cade. All six-foot, one-hundred-eighty pounds of lean, gorgeous male standing at her doorstep. He looked big and rumpled and so sexy that he stole her breath.

Take another deep, even breath, she told herself.

She didn't need this. Didn't want her hormones to go berserk at the sight of a man she'd always considered off-limits. Plenty of other women chased him. Why couldn't he be satisfied with his current collection of lady friends? Most of them were attractive and personable. Why had his attention suddenly shifted to her?

Years of polite social conditioning came in handy, but it still took every ounce of courage she could marshal to open the door and face him.

She wasn't sure what to expect, but it wasn't the slow, steady perusal he gave her. It was entirely too intimate, too knowing, too disturbingly male. A blush scorched her face and neck as he searched her features. When his gaze dropped, her nipples immediately beaded against the silk, pouting for attention. Additional heat swelled in her breasts and arrowed down to her belly when his gaze drifted the length of her.

The man was a menace. Her experience with sex was woefully limited, and he agitated her beyond belief. She didn't have a clue about dealing with what they'd just shared. There were no safe, sane guidelines to follow, personally or professionally.

Words failed her.

"Can I come in?" His tone was polite, belying the fact that they'd just been about as intimate as two people could get while fully clothed.

She didn't reply, but opened the door wider and stepped aside to give him space. Still, the scent and heat of him made her acutely aware of her own femininity. She ignored her skittering pulse, turned her back to the door as she closed it, and watched him pace her living room. He seemed as unnerved as she, so she just waited.

"I owe you an apology, and I think you owe me one, too," he finally said, his dark gaze latching onto hers.

Surprised, she arched a brow. Cautiously, she asked, "What exactly are you apologizing for?"

"For grabbing you in anger." His expression and tone were fierce as he spoke. He ran his fingers through already-ravaged hair. "I deliberately goaded you into a temper and then took advantage of you."

So the provocation had been intentional.

He pierced her with a penetrating gaze. "That's all I'm apologizing for. I'm not the least bit sorry for anything that followed."

"It was scandalous and unprofessional." She almost choked on the words. "It never should have happened."

A frown creased his forehead. "You're wrong about that. Dead wrong. The time and place might have been better, but not our actions. I don't regret one second of it."

More heat suffused Sallie's body as their gazes tangled again. She knew him well enough to know he meant what he said. Of course, he hadn't been the one who'd experienced a wanton lack of control.

Her breasts tingled with remembered sensations, so she crossed her arms over her chest. Cade was wrong. That sort of interlude might be common for him, but it had really distressed her. They hadn't just broken the rules of professional decorum, they'd obliterated them.

When she didn't respond, he asked, "Do you regret making love with me?"

"Of course I do," she insisted, but she couldn't maintain eye contact. Her heart and head were having a clash of wills. Right now, her brain had control. Barely. "It shouldn't have happened. We had a perfect working relationship. We're a good team. We've worked so hard for so long, yet you seem willing to throw that all away for a little sexual dalliance."

"Dalliance?" His tone went dangerously soft, a sure sign that her words infuriated him. "If you call that a dalliance, sweetheart, your sex life must be a helluva lot more interesting than mine. I call it the sweetest lovemaking I've ever known."

His declaration sent fire through her veins, arousing and confusing her at the same time. He had to have shared a lot more with a lot of women. Blushing and stuttering and hating herself for both, Sallie tried to make sense of it all. "But you didn't...didn't even...how could...?"

Taking a deep breath, she tried again. "How could it have been good for you?"

Cade groaned, closed his eyes and turned his back on her. "Let's not go there right now, okay?" He sounded as though he still hadn't fully recovered. "I'd like to explain it sometime, but not while there's so much other garbage between us. We have more immediate problems."

"For instance?"

He turned and glared at her again. "Your resignation. I'm not accepting it. And you still owe me that apology. Not to mention a detailed explanation for five years of deceit."

For a long moment, they continued to stare at each other, their tension a living, breathing thing.

Then Sallie sighed heavily. She did owe him that much. He'd hired her in good faith, and had trusted her from the start. There'd been times over the years when her conscience had pricked, but she'd never found the right time or words to confess. Surely they could discuss the problem like two civilized adults. Maybe even get past the disturbing twist their relationship had taken.

"Why don't you have a seat? I'm thirsty," she said, turning toward the kitchen. "Would you like something to drink?"

"Got a beer?"

"No."

"Just as well. Alcohol might not be a good idea."

"Iced tea? Juice? Cola?"

"Whatever you're having is fine."

He started to take a seat, but accidentally stepped on Jasper's squeaky toy. Jas shot out from under the sofa, snatched the toy with a vicious snarl, and then disappeared again in a blur of fur.

"What the hell?"

Sallie raised her voice to explain from the kitchen. "That was my cat, Jasper. He's not very sociable, so he probably won't make another appearance. He's just spastic about that old stuffed snake."

"You have an obsessive, spastic cat, and we didn't even catch sight of him the other night?"

"He's not much of a guard cat. He hides from strangers."

"Even prowlers?"

"He stayed under my bed until everyone was gone," she said, carrying two glasses of iced tea back to the living room. "Maybe what I really need is a big, ugly watchdog."

"Or you could tell me the truth. The whole truth. And let me and Steven up your security."

She handed him a glass, being careful not to touch him in the process. Then she eased herself into a chair opposite him.

"I told you the truth."

"That your father is filthy rich and you had to hide your identity to get a regular job? I'm guessing you wanted to establish a reputation on your own merit. I can understand that. I'm not sure how I would have responded if you'd told me that five years ago," he admitted. "But my reaction couldn't have been the only factor in your secrecy. You had already changed your identity by the time you applied at Langden's."

Sallie took a long, soothing drink of tea, enjoying the coolness as it slid down her throat. "That's about the extent of it. I craved normalcy, and knew I'd never have it unless I could become anonymous."

"And how did you accomplish that? Didn't your folks object? How could you erase your past?"

"My parents raised me in a very insular world. There wasn't much past to hide."

"You told me they were retired and living in Florida."

"Semi-retired and it's Arizona. My dad won't fully retire until the day he dies. He invented the term workaholic."

"You're completely estranged?"

"No, not at all," Sallie shook her head. "I talk to them and visit once in a while, but they're still jet setting around the world on a regular basis. I never cared for that sort of lifestyle."

"And he's never wanted you to follow in his footsteps?"

She licked her lips, but then noticed how intently he watched her every move. It flustered her. "Of course he does. He'd hand me the whole empire if I wanted it," she grumbled, "as long as I didn't expect him to actually relinquish control."

She adored her father, but could never work with him. "I'll always be his little girl, regardless of my business savvy and executive titles."

"No siblings to share all that adoration?"

Sallie's pulse leapt briefly, and then she frowned at how the question still had the power to hurt her. Even after all the years. Her throat tightened. "I had a big brother, Brent. He was two years older and my hero, but he died when I was thirteen."

Tears threatened, proof of how emotionally fragile she was feeling. She hadn't cried for Brent in years. She didn't look directly at Cade, but could almost hear him thinking, remembering.

"Kidnapped and murdered," he whispered softly. "Now I remember. The Harrimans had a son who was kidnapped from their Long Island home. I was just a teenager. I didn't pay much attention to the details back then, but I remember it made national news for a few weeks."

Sallie nodded. It had been a nightmarish time for her family. After Brent's death, her parents had been almost maniacal in their efforts to protect her. She'd missed her brother horribly, grieved for him, and become a virtual prisoner in her own home.

"That's why your parents agreed to a change of identity? Steven said enough money and clout could probably get the job done."

"Steven and my parents are in agreement on that," she said. "There's very little their money can't buy. But they couldn't buy Brent's safety, so they agreed to help me disassociate myself from the Harriman name."

"Your idea or theirs?"

She gave him an admonishing look. "The idea was mine, and it wasn't very popular. My dad finally conceded, with conditions. He views his capitulation as a strategic maneuver, giving me a little rope to hang myself, so to speak. He's betting I'll weary of an average lifestyle, come to my senses and then be more malleable."

Cade laughed, and the sound rippled over her like a caress. "He just doesn't get it, huh?"

The pride in his eyes unnerved her as little else could have done. She didn't want to be warmed from head-to-toe by his empathy. She'd always kept her professional and private lives separate, but he kept tangling them up.

"My dad thrives on his lifestyle, and he loves me. He can't accept the fact that I don't think, feel and act exactly the way he wants."

"How about your mother?"

She smiled. "Mother would prefer to have me in her social sphere, but she's a wise woman. She knows how to let go. She wants me to have my heart's desire."

"And what is it? Your heart's desire?"

His tone had gone husky, his gaze penetrating. Sallie felt like squirming under the intensity of his regard. She had no intention of sharing her hopes and dreams with him. He'd think her crazy. Most people would. An heiress to billions who wanted a white picket fence, 2.5 children and an everyday hero?

"Can I get you some more tea?" she asked, declaring the subject taboo.

"No thanks," he set his empty glass on the table. "What I'd like is more information. Like who's stalking you, what it does or doesn't have to do with Langden's, and why you refused more protection."

Happy to redirect the conversation, she said, "When I changed identities, I swore I'd never be paranoid about safety again. I don't want bodyguards or twenty-four-hour-a-day surveillance. I don't want to be a prisoner in my own home."

Her fingers tightened on her glass. "I shouldn't have to be. I've had my fill of it," she argued heatedly, and then forced herself to calm down a little. "As for the other, I've been trying to figure out a connection, but I don't see it."

"Is there a chance this stalker knows who you really are?"

A shiver raced over her at the suggestion. It wasn't the first time the thought had entered her mind. "I guess it's possible, but it doesn't make sense. He doesn't threaten me, and he never mentions the business or my background."

"What does he say then?"

Her cheeks grew warm again. "Mostly, he just says things about the way I look or act on any given day. About how hard I work, and how nice it would be to share time with me."

Cade's voice went cold and harsh. "He wants intimacy?"

"That's the usual tone, but he's never overtly suggestive. Never lewd or threatening."

"He's never suggested that the two of you meet?"

She shook her head. "He acts like we're old friends or something."

"Old lovers?"

"I guess that's an accurate assessment of his attitude," she said, running a finger along the rim of her glass. "The police went with that angle, but I can assure you it's not the case. I don't have a string of ex-lovers."

"It's not the sort of thing your dad would do to force you back home, is it?"

"Never," she insisted vehemently, shaking her head. "My dad would never stoop to that kind of trick. He may be ruthless in his business dealings, but he'd never deliberately scare me."

"Someone from your old life who wants to exploit you?"

Sallie thought of Derrick. He'd wanted to marry into the Harriman empire, but he'd destroyed his chances and nearly landed in jail. He'd quickly married another rich girl to save his hide. Shaking her head again, she said, "I've given it a lot of thought, and I just can't think of anyone."

"Have the calls stopped?"

"I just got the privacy screening system on my phone, so I hope that's the end of them. It rejects calls from untraceable numbers. Hopefully, he'll lose interest in me altogether."

She hated to think he'd direct his interest to some other innocent woman, but it was beyond her control.

"He'll be annoyed, that's for sure. First, we removed his bugs and secured your house and then we thwarted his efforts to contact you by phone. He'll either be discouraged or enraged. I don't like to think about the latter."

She didn't like it, either. Putting up with an unwanted admirer was a little less terrifying than having an angry, deranged stalker.

"You could let Steven arrange a little more protection."

Sallie glared at him. "I'd prefer to believe the man has lost interest. I've updated the security around here, and I'm trying to be more cautious."

Cade nodded, apparently satisfied with her response. She sighed a little and checked the time.

"You really shouldn't miss that appointment with Carl Anderson this afternoon," she said.

He glanced at his watch and then her. "I told Steven to cancel everything, but I might be able to reschedule. Anxious to be rid of me?"

"Just minding your business."

It took all her strength to keep from squirming under his intense perusal. She continued to hold his gaze.

"You are a first-class assistant," he said as he rose to his feet. "Don't expect me to accept your resignation."

Sallie rose to her feet, and led him back to the door. Encouraged by their ability to converse like two reasonable adults, she decided that maybe they could get past the incident at the office.

"I've always loved my job, and I don't want to leave."

"But?" he asked, as she reached for the doorknob, then paused and turned to him again.

"But I want your promise that we keep our relationship strictly professional."

Tension instantly sprang between them, fierce and palpable. It became a force to reckon with. Sallie's breath caught at the ferocity of Cade's expression.

"I'm not sure what the hell upset you, but you still owe me an apology and an explanation."

Her breathing faltered. Keeping her tone light, she asked, "For what, exactly?"

"First, you can apologize for that cheap shot about revenge."

Heat singed her neck and cheeks again. Lowering her lashes didn't completely block out the sight of his tight expression. She'd thrown that insult at him in self-defense, to cover her own distress and vulnerability. She really didn't believe it.

"Sorry about that," she said, a wave of heat rolling over her at the reminder.

Cade relaxed a little and his tone grew softer. "Apology accepted. Now maybe you'd like to explain why you were so upset about what we shared."

That made her eyes widen as she stared at him in astonishment. "You honestly don't understand?"

The slow, steady shake of his head had her mentally scrambling for an explanation.

"It was highly unprofessional."

"We can't neatly compartmentalize every aspect of our lives. Sometimes the private and professional get scrambled. They're both parts of our whole."

Sallie didn't want her self-imposed boundaries to get blurred. As far as she was concerned, Cade had always belonged within the professional realm. She had difficulty thinking about him in a personal fashion.

At least she did until his eyes got all heavy with warmth and invitation, like they were right now. She'd seen a lot of expressions cross his face over the years—pride, anger, exhilaration. But she'd never had the deep, dark sensuality directed at her. It made her knees weak.

He reached a hand out, and she flinched. Then he stepped closer to cup her face. She dropped her lashes to hide her reaction as heat shimmered through her, reigniting barely tamped fires.

"I'm a toucher." He offered an explanation, not an apology. His thumb stroked her cheek, so gently, so seductively. Every nerve in her body responded. "I enjoy the skin-to-skin contact, the feel of a woman."

"I'm not very comfortable with touching," she said, and then contradicted the statement by rubbing her cheek against his hand.

"You don't like it?" he asked quietly.

She liked it too much. Way too much. She could easily become addicted. He made her feel like purring with satisfaction. They were treading dangerous waters again, and she was floundering in sensation. It might be everyday male-female interaction for him, but she was way out of her depth.

She lifted her lashes and stared into the rich, caramel warmth of his eyes. She saw curiosity mingled with hunger and just a little of the confusion she knew was reflected in her eyes. "It just complicates things," she whispered.

"And you don't think it's worth the complication?"

"I don't know."

"Then maybe we should find out."

Her breath caught in her throat. "Or maybe, if we ignore it, it'll go away."

Cade shook his head again, but his gaze stayed locked with hers. "It's not going away. It's too intense, too urgent."

"You're sure?"

Now he nodded affirmatively, his gaze dropping to her mouth as his thumb strayed to her lips. He had far more experience than she. He'd probably known all levels of sexual desire, so she had to assume he was right about the chemistry between them. Once they'd tested the volatile nature of it, it wasn't likely to dissipate.

"So, what now? An office affair that will have all the gossips salivating? I don't think I can work in that kind of environment. It's too demeaning."

"I promise not to jump your bones at work," he teased, tugging her a little closer. "I'll do my best to keep my hands to myself, but I still want you there working with me. We're a team. Have been from the start."

Sallie sighed, momentarily allowing her body to rest against the fascinating hardness of his. Then she nodded agreement. She didn't want to leave Langden Industries. They'd created a company to be proud of, but she didn't know how they were supposed to deal with all the sexual tension.

The question must have been obvious by her expression, because Cade offered a solution. "Why don't we go away for a while and explore the private side of our relationship?"

"Go away?" The words snagged in her throat.

"Go somewhere for a few days, and get to know each other outside of the office."

Was he talking about a brief, passionate affair? She cut to the bottom line. "You're thinking that we can get this out of our systems if we spend some time alone?"

He frowned, and his gaze sharpened. "That's not what I'm thinking at all. Why are you so eager to write this off as a temporary blip in our lives?" he demanded irritably.

"Maybe because you've had a lot of women in your life over the years. None of them lasted very long."

His mouth tightened. "I don't discard my friends."

"No, but lovers come in and out of favor."

"And you think you're just a passing fancy?" he asked, snatching his hand from her face.

The truth might annoy him, but he couldn't deny it, nor could she. Where would they be once the passion faded? Could they still be friends as well as business associates? He might want her now. That didn't mean he wanted a long-term relationship. The question was, was she willing to settle for anything else?

"Are you afraid to test it?" he asked.

She twisted the doorknob and pulled the door open, then turned and looked him directly in the eyes.

"I honestly don't know. It's tempting, but I'll have to give it some thought."

Her answer didn't satisfy him, but he accepted it with a nod. He strode through the door.

"You'll be at the office in the morning?"

"I'll give it serious consideration."

Chapter Seven

Sallie fully intended to be early for work the next morning. She wanted to be settled in her own private domain before the rest of the staff arrived. There'd be speculation as to why she left in such a temper, and she wanted it all to die a natural death.

She overslept for the first time in years, probably due to a restless night. Then she changed clothes three times before settling on a no-frills lavender suit that was plain and businesslike. She didn't want to be accused of wearing anything sexy or provocative. Soft and feminine were out, too.

The uncharacteristic waffling about clothes made her irritable as well as tardy. She left the house half an hour later than planned, then realized her car had a flat tire.

Glancing around, she noticed that none of her neighbors seemed to be stirring. The sky was cloudy and the early morning darkness hadn't lightened yet. The streetlights illuminated the area a little, but the silence was eerie.

"Damn it to hell," she muttered. Snatching her cell phone, she called directory assistance for a local service station. Punching in that number, she was told that it might take as long as an hour for someone to get there.

"So much for keeping to a normal, dignified routine," she said to herself, heading back to the house. She'd have to cool her heels until the repair truck arrived. And she needed to call the office before Cade started hunting her down.

Jasper greeted her with a mewing welcome even though she hadn't been gone more than a couple minutes. He jumped to the back of a chair, and she patted his head while using the phone. The office answering machine clicked, telling her that nobody had arrived to switch it over to manual operation.

She dialed Cade's private office line, but got no answer there, either. Thinking that she needed more caffeine, she went to the kitchen and brewed another pot of coffee. Ten minutes later, she carried her cup into the living room and glanced out the front window. A tow truck was pulling into her driveway.

"Well, Jas, it looks like the day might be improving already." She set down her coffee and grabbed her purse.

"That was fast," she said to the man who climbed from the truck. "Your station said it might take an hour."

"In the area," he mumbled as he walked to the rear of her car and kicked the flat tire. "You got roadside assistance? Otherwise, I'll need cash up front."

Dressed from head to toe in a brown uniform with a matching hat pulled low over his forehead, he reminded Sallie of a tree trunk. She only gave him a curious glance before digging her identification card from her purse. She tried to hand it to him, but he waved her away.

"Later," he mumbled again.

She watched from a distance of a few yards as he jacked the car up, loosened the lug nuts, and efficiently replaced the flat tire with a new one. He seemed to know his business, so she didn't bother him.

The job was nearly finished when she heard her phone ringing inside. Almost simultaneously, her cell phone rang. She pulled it from her purse while she headed back into the house.

"Sallie, it's Cade."

Why didn't that surprise her?

"Good morning, Cade. I was heading into work, but I'm having a little difficulty getting there."

"What kind of difficulty?" The sharpness of his question had her pausing mid-stride. Then she continued in to the house in time to hear Steven leaving a message on her machine.

"Sallie, there's been more trouble. Call me as soon as possible."

"Sallie?" Cade's voice rang in her ear as Steven's faded into silence.

She dropped her purse on the floor. "I'm sorry, I just walked back in the house and heard Steven's message about more trouble. What's happening?"

"There was a break-in at the office. I'm headed there now, but I'm swinging by your place first."

"That's not necessary. I had a flat tire, but someone came to fix it already."

"Who? Don't let anybody in the house and don't go outside alone!" he growled. "I'll be there in a couple minutes."

The phone went dead, and Sallie shook her head in consternation. She could get really annoyed with his protective attitude. Still, she closed and locked the door behind her, then moved to the window. Within a few minutes, she saw Cade's pickup turn onto her street.

Surprisingly, the tow truck backed out of her drive at the same time, speeding down the street before Cade pulled into her drive.

"What the heck?" she wondered, heading back outside, feeling like some kind of puppet on a string.

Cade swung out of his truck and they met in her driveway.

"You okay?"

"I'm fine. Why shouldn't I be? He left without payment," she said, staring down the street. "I didn't even give him my auto card."

Cade's expression was fierce, this jaw taut with anger. "I think you might have just met your stalker," he said with a low, fierce growl.

The suggestion shocked her and sent a shiver down her spine. "How can that be? I picked a service station at random." She went on to explain exactly what had transpired after she'd noticed the flat.

"Did he show any ID or give you the name of the station?"

"No, now that you mention it. But how would he know I had a flat tire?"

"He'd know if he was the one who flattened it."

A shudder raced over her. Just then, another truck pulled onto the street. It bore the logo of a local service station.

"Ohmigod," she whispered, lifting a hand to her mouth as the whole situation began to sink in. Someone had flattened her tire, watched until she'd called for help, and then pretended to come to her aid. And for what? Her stomach knotted.

What had he hoped to accomplish? Was this his way of bypassing her increased security? Had her phone calls from Cade and Steven saved her from whatever he'd intended?

"Stay put." Cade headed out to meet the other serviceman. The two men talked briefly, and then he returned to her side.

"What's going on now?"

"I can drive you to work. I've asked him to change your tire again and put on the one you ordered. Steven can check out the one your impostor put on while he checks the rest of the car for problems."

Sallie glanced at her midsized gray sedan. "You don't think he damaged my car, do you?"

"No, but he could have installed another bug, a tracking device or worse."

"Worse?"

Cade didn't answer, but his expression was grim. The only other thing she could think of was a bomb. Her eyes went wide at the thought.

Then he grabbed her forearms and pulled her close for a kiss. His mouth was hard and demanding, his body equally hard. She leaned into him, briefly savoring the heat, strength and comfort. When she offered no resistance, his mouth gradually softened, coaxing a deeper response from her. Her lips parted, inviting his tongue inside to slide seductively against hers.

After the kiss, he wrapped his arms around her and held her tightly for a few minutes, resting his face in her hair. She tucked her face into his neck, relishing the contact. Then she remembered where they were and pulled back.

"You promised," she scolded huskily.

"I promised not to kiss you at the office," he clarified. "That one was as necessary as my next breath."

Sallie slowly shook her head. Could he have needed the reassurance as much as she had? How could she resist a man who knew exactly what she needed when she needed it? The kiss had helped her regain her equilibrium and shake off the insidious fear caused by an unknown stalker.

Cade walked with her to the house to collect her purse and briefcase. He watched as she locked the door and followed her back outside again.

"Steven called me about more trouble. Is that why you called, too? Why you came past my house?"

"Yeah," he explained as he guided her to his truck, and then helped her into the passenger seat. "We had a break-in at the office last night. Steven called me as soon as he got there this morning, then we called both your numbers."

"How bad was it?"

He climbed into the driver's seat, put the truck in gear and backed out of her driveway. "Steven said there wasn't much damage. It looks more like random vandalism. Some papers thrown around, drawers pulled out, a few small items broken. He can't tell if anything's missing, so we'll have to sort through the mess and see what we can find."

"You think it has something to do with my stalker?"

"I think it's a good possibility."

He sounded as troubled as she felt. "And the point of the vandalism?"

Cade shot her an assessing glance, and then turned his attention to the traffic. "To keep Steven and I occupied while he came after you."

Sallie bit her lip, fighting back an unwelcome surge of panic. The man in brown hadn't seemed threatening or dangerous. What was he after? Had he planned to abduct her? If so, why hadn't he done anything while it was still relatively dark outside? Why hadn't she paid more attention?

So many questions and no answers.

Within twenty minutes, they'd reached the office building and taken the elevator to the twelfth floor. They presented a calm, united front as they entered Langden's outer offices and faced the concerns of their staff.

The reception area and bookkeeping departments hadn't been too badly damaged. The staff slowly arrived for work and offered to help with cleaning, but nothing could be done until an insurance investigator catalogued the damages.

Steven met them in Sallie's office. He and the police detective had already gone over the whole place. They opted not to call in an evidence team since nothing had been stolen and they didn't expect to find any fingerprints. All they could do was take photos of the damage and file another report.

Cade's office took the brunt of the vandal's malice. Furniture was sliced, pictures smashed and documents shredded. His computer had been bashed along with most of the other electronic equipment.

"Looks like our vandal vented a little extra frustration in your office, Mr. Langden," commented the detective. "Know anybody with a grudge?"

Cade glanced at Sallie. "My guess is a stalker with an attitude. He probably resents my intervention in Sallie's personal security."

They briefly outlined what had happened at her house. The detective asked more questions, took notes and eventually turned the crime scene over to the insurance investigator. Since their insurance agency was located in the same building, the investigation was swift and thorough. After an hour or so, he gave them permission to start clearing the clutter.

Cade and Sallie worked together to back up computer files and make copies of all their most important documents. Lunch was ordered for the entire staff while everyone worked to right their areas. By late afternoon, they'd ordered new equipment and were ready to turn the office over to a cleaning crew.

"It's going to take the rest of the week to get the place cleaned and everything replaced," said Cade. "I've cleared my calendar, and I'm heading home for a really long weekend. Want to come with me?"

Sallie glanced at him in surprise. He rarely took time off during their busy season. He'd never invited her or, to her knowledge, any other woman to his family ranch near Albuquerque.

"Won't Trey and Jillian mind your bringing an unexpected guest home with you?" she asked, worrying about his brother and sister-in-law's reaction if they just showed up on their doorstep.

"They're taking Eli to Disney World this week. Trey asked if I had time to hang out at the ranch, but I told him no. I've changed my mind."

"You don't have to take me anywhere for protection," she argued, although, right now, the idea of running away and hiding held great appeal.

He studied her face, his expression never changing. "The truth is I'm sick of the city and sick of people right now. Spending time at the ranch always helps me get life back into perspective."

That made sense to Sallie, but she didn't want to intrude on his private time nor transfer her troubles to his sanctuary. "Then go, I'll take care of things here."

He moved closer and cupped her cheek in his hand. After the briefest of caresses, he jerked it back to his side, belatedly remembering his promise.

His eyes clouded with intensity as he continued. "I want you with me. I want to share the serenity. There's so much to show you, and it won't hurt to disappear for a few days. Let your stalker stew about that while Steven and the police try to determine his identity."

Even though he talked about the stalker and protecting her, Sallie understood his unspoken intentions. He wanted them to become lovers. He'd left no doubt about that. The fact sizzled between them as they continued to stare at each other. She could feel the desire arcing between his body and hers. If she agreed to accompany him, she'd be agreeing to an affair.

Steven flew them to Albuquerque in a company jet, and then Cade rented a pickup truck for the final drive to the Langden ranch. Flying always exhausted Sallie, yet she still surprised herself by sleeping most of the two-hour drive. She woke to the feel of Cade brushing her hair from her face. He'd parked the truck and shut off the engine, but a nearby security light allowed her to see his features. His expression held so much tenderness that her breath caught in her throat.

Her pulse quickened. "Cade?"

"Sallie," he whispered, dropping his head to press a gentle kiss on her lips. "We're home."

The intimacy of his tone and words sent a shiver of delicious sensation through her body. She straightened in her seat, lifting herself closer to him. Cade reached across to release her seatbelt and the brush of his arms against her breasts sent heat licking through her veins. He drew her closer and his next kiss nearly melted every bone in her body. She didn't know how he managed to convey so much emotion in a kiss.

So hot. So needy. So persuasive.

His tongue explored her mouth with a thoroughness that wiped all thought from her mind. As the thoughts flew out, emotion surged in, pulsing between them like a wild, untamed beast. His arms tightened, gathering her closer. She slid her arms around his waist and clung to him as if he were her only anchor in a storm.

A series of long, deep kisses left them both panting for air. "I'd better get you inside or I might embarrass myself by losing control in the cab of a truck," he managed on a gruff whisper. Holding her face between his hands, he gazed into her passion-clouded eyes. "Would that totally shock you?"

Sallie licked her lips. He groaned, making her heart beat a little faster, but she tried to answer him as honestly as possible. "I might be a little shocked. Nobody has ever tried to seduce me in a truck before."

"You never experimented with sex in the backseat of a car or the bed of a pickup truck? I thought that was a rite of passage for all teenagers."

Sallie thought of her one and only experiment with sex. It hadn't been in a vehicle and it hadn't been pleasant. "During my teenage years, I rarely went anywhere without a chaperone and usually a bodyguard or two," she reminded him.

"Ah, I forgot," he said softly. "Sometime I'll teach you the basics, but I promise you didn't miss much. Tight spaces are okay for having sex, but not that good for making love."

Sallie searched his features and saw only sincerity. It both pleased and alarmed her that he wanted more than sex from her. She liked the idea of making love even if they weren't in love with each other, but she feared it could be too easy to fall in love with a man who differentiated between the two. On top of that worry, she also worried about her own inexperience. She really had no idea how to make love to a man as sensual and passionate as Cade. Would he find her ineptness too boring to bear?

"What brought that frown to your pretty face?" he asked.

Sallie shook her head, unwilling to voice her concerns. "I guess I'm still a little groggy," she said, straightening in her seat.

She felt his gaze for a few seconds longer, but then he climbed out of the cab without another word. He pulled their suitcases from the rear seat of the club cab and came around to open her door. She grabbed her pocketbook and overnight bag. They both had their hands full, so she followed him as he made his way onto the house's wraparound porch. He paused to collect a hidden key and unlocked the door, pushing it wide for her to enter. Sallie stepped into a wide, well-lit foyer.

"When I called to let Trey know we were coming, Jillian said she hoped the place didn't smell stale from being closed up a few days. They left last Friday."

Sallie smelled scented candles or potpourri. "More like lilacs," she said, wondering exactly what Cade had told his family. "Did Trey and Jillian know I was coming with you?"

She watched his eyes narrow as they pinned her in a stare.

"Ashamed for them to know you're here with me?" he asked tightly.

She found the courage to return his stare. "Not ashamed, but definitely out of my element," she confessed. Her tone grew defensive. "I might as well be totally honest and warn you that I have no experience in sexual relationships."

Cade dropped their suitcases with a thud and propped his hands on his hips.

"Could you be a little more specific with your warning?"

"I've never had a lover." The confession came out more breathy than she liked.

A low groan escaped him. "Please don't tell me you're a virgin."

"Would that be so horrible?" she asked, frowning.

He grimaced and ran a hand over his face. "No, it's not horrible. It's fine, just fine, but a man needs to know these things."

Sallie's wariness turned to annoyance. "Well, relax. I'm not a virgin, so you don't have to panic. I just don't have as much experience as you do."

Some of the tension drained from him, but his gaze grew speculative. "How much sexual experience are we talking about here?"

She hedged. "Mine or yours?"

Cade's eyes narrowed. "Yours."

"I've had sex."

"Do you mind if I ask how much sex?"

"Yes, I mind."

"Don't you think I have a right to know if we're going to be lovers?"

She dropped her bags and crossed her arms over her chest. "You want to swap stories and numbers?" she taunted.

"No," he snapped. "I just want to know how long it's been since you had sex. That's important in case I need to be careful."

Sallie felt a blush heating her cheeks and avoided his question with one of her own. "How long has it been for you?" she asked.

"Six months," he said.

"Six years," she tossed back at him.

"Six years!" His shout was so loud that Sallie cringed. She hoped nobody on the property could hear him.

"And if that's not shocking enough, I've only had one partner," she grumbled. It would make things easier in the long run if Cade knew the depth of her inexperience, but she really didn't want to talk about it. Her one and only sexual encounter had been so humiliating she didn't like to think about it, let alone discuss it with another man.

He just stared at her for a long minute, and she desperately wished she could read his mind. "If you have a problem with that, I can find my own way back to Dallas," she offered.

"Hell, no," he said, shaking his head. "I didn't mean to make you uncomfortable. I'm just surprised. I've seen so many men drooling over you in the past five years that I assumed you had a pretty active social life."

"Active doesn't mean promiscuous."

He shook his head again and shoved the door closed. "Why do I get the feeling you're itching for a fight?" he asked, turning to her again. "Are you sorry you agreed to come with me?"

Sallie sighed and thought about the kiss they'd just shared. She badly wanted to explore the chemistry between them. She cared deeply for Cade, and he stirred her senses as no other man had ever done. She didn't want to leave. She wanted to stay here with him and delve into that heated desire.

She captured his gaze with her own. "I guess I'm just a little stressed about the whole situation."

He studied her face intently. She couldn't tell whether her words pacified him or not, but some of the tension drained from his expression.

"We've both had a long day and a rough few weeks. Let me show you to your room, and then we'll get something to eat."

He led her through the house, pointing out the formal living room, family room and dining room as they made their way to a suite of bedrooms in the west wing. When they passed his bedroom, he flipped on the light, illuminating a blend of navy blue and gold that shrieked of masculinity. Just the thought of sharing the king-sized bed with him sent a shiver down her spine.

The décor of the adjoining room had a softer mix of beiges and greens. Cade set down her suitcase near a four-poster bed covered with a patchwork quilt.

"We share a bathroom," he explained, pointing to a door to the right of the bed. "These are the only two downstairs bedrooms. If you want more privacy, you can have a room upstairs."

His offer made her feel like a naïve twit. She hadn't come all this way to distance herself from her would-be lover. She'd never shared a bathroom with anyone in her whole life, but she'd bite off her tongue before admitting it.

"This is fine, thank you."

Cade visibly relaxed, making her realize how tense they'd both gotten. She wanted to get back some of their normal, easy rapport. "How about something to eat? I'm starving and you did promise me food."

He gave her a totally wicked, totally gorgeous grin that sent a ripple of response over her nerves.

"I'm not even sure what's on hand, but I reckon I can scrounge up something to satisfy your needs," he said with a wink.

Sallie ignored the double-entendre even though it sent heat coursing through her veins. "You reckon?" she teased.

"I reckon," he reiterated as he directed her to the kitchen at the back of the house. "That's cowboy talk."

"I never would have guessed."

"That's 'cause you're a city girl," he explained in a slow drawl.

"That I am," she admitted.

His playfulness set the tone for the next hour. Together they raided the refrigerator and put together a light meal, keeping things equally light between them. Cade put her at ease so effortlessly that Sallie found herself wondering how often he'd done the same thing with other women. He did a lot of entertaining at his bachelor pad in Dallas, but she wondered how often he'd brought a woman to his childhood home.

She also wondered if those other encounters ended with wild, untamed sex in the kitchen. On the table? Against the countertop? In the middle of the floor? She'd read romance novels that went into great detail about such encounters. They'd made her extremely curious, yet she lacked the courage to initiate the foreplay. She appreciated a woman's right to take charge of the physical aspect of a relationship, but she decided to leave that part to Cade.

Feeling herself blush at the wild direction of her thoughts, she finished off her portion of the omelet with her head dipped and her gaze fixed on the plate.

Chapter Eight

Cade thought he deserved a medal for not seducing Sallie while they'd moved around the kitchen. He enjoyed every minute of time with her and wanted her to be comfortable with him on a very personal level. He hadn't wanted to rush her, but each brush of her body against his had kicked his temperature a little higher. Every whiff of her unique perfume had tantalized his senses. The sound of her soft laughter kept the blood churning through his body. He couldn't remember ever hungering after a woman so intensely. She'd become a fever in his blood that he couldn't cool, and he could barely control.

He'd been the gentleman and given her first turn in the bathroom. He paced his room, trying not to invade her privacy by straining to hear every move she made. Still, he couldn't help envisioning her tall, slender body naked and glistening in the shower. It took all his considerable willpower to stay on his side of the bathroom door.

When she called out that she'd finished, Cade shucked his clothes and grabbed a clean pair of boxers. Considering Sallie's inexperience, he'd decided to let her set the pace of things. Determined to get through the rest of the night without pouncing on his guest, he promised himself a cold shower and stepped into the bathroom.

All his blood rushed to his groin as a steamy cloud of light intoxicating perfume enveloped him. The desire he'd tried to ignore all evening socked him in the gut and the erection that had been at half-staff turned to stone. He groaned, inhaling deeply as the scent of Sallie seeped into every pore of his body.

He wanted more. A whole helluva lot more. What he allowed himself was a frigid shower that did little to cool his jets. Goose bumps covered his wrinkling skin before he finally turned off the taps and stepped from the stall. Chilled, but feeling more in control, he grabbed a towel.

As he roughly dried himself, he noticed there wasn't any visible sign Sallie had shared the bathroom. In her usual, super-organized fashion, she'd left the room as neat and clean as it had been before she used it. The woman really needed to learn how to be less than perfect, he thought, knotting the towel at his waist.

He glanced at the clean underwear he'd brought with him, but didn't reach for them. He'd just peek into her room, and see if she'd fallen asleep. If she'd settled for the night, he'd do the same. After turning off the light, he reached for the door to her room, wondering if she'd locked it. The knob turned soundlessly, sending a shiver of relief over him. Maybe it wasn't the brazen invitation he'd have liked, but at least Sallie wasn't erecting barriers between them.

It took a minute for his eyes to adjust to the shadowed darkness. A faint gleam of moonlight spilled across the bed. He could see Sallie's slim shape beneath a cotton sheet. Her hair spilled across the pillowcase and the pale skin of her bare shoulders glistened in the dimness. His heart kicked into high gear at the sight of her. His body started to throb again, this time harder and hotter than before. The erection that had softened in the shower sprang to stiffness beneath the towel.

"Sallie?" Her name escaped in gravelly roughness.

Her voice came back to him, whisper soft. "Cade."

"Calling it a night?" he forced himself to ask, and then held his breath as several heartbeats passed before her response.

"Waiting for you."

Her breathless admission sent a shudder over him, destroying all thoughts of chivalry. He watched, mesmerized, as she used her feet to slowly drag the sheet from her shoulders, exposing pale flesh that glowed in the moonlight. Slowly, inch-by-achingly-slow-inch, the shifting sheet bared more gleaming skin, and he realized she must be naked, gloriously, excitingly nude beneath the sheet, and she was prepared to torture him with a slow strip tease.

Cade's breath hitched, the air clogging his lungs. His chest tightened with vice-like pressure until he forgot to breathe at all. When she uncovered her rounded breasts with their plump, stiff nipples, all the air whooshed out of him in a panting rush. He nearly hyperventilated when the sheet continued to slide across the dip of her waist and then the curve of her hips.

She wanted him. His pulse jumped at her bold way of getting the message across to him. The baring of her body was the indisputable invitation he'd badly needed.

When the sheet stopped just short of her mound, he realized he wasn't breathing at all. His lungs stung, so he sucked air into them again. Need coursed through him in a rush of hot, heavy anticipation as he moved toward her on legs that were none too sturdy.

He wanted to switch on a light so he could see and explore every inch of her lovely body. His fingers flexed and his muscles bunched in eagerness. Then he remembered her inexperience and natural modesty. He didn't think her boldness would stretch that far this first time. That was okay. He could get to know her more intimately through touch and scent anyway.

The towel slid from his waist, but he hardly noticed as he made his way across the room. He watched Sallie's eyes widen as she let her gaze roam over him. He wouldn't have thought it possible, but his arousal intensified with craving. His whole body pulsed with the heavy cadence of blood flowing to his groin.

By the time her perusal had drifted back up his body, he'd reached her side. Their gazes locked, and he knew his eyes mirrored the dark, swirling passion in hers. For a long, heated moment, he soaked up the fascinating beauty of her expression—the liquid beauty of her eyes, the softly parted lips, and the expression of surrender he'd only seen in his dreams.

When Cade finally tore his gaze from her face, he looked down at the beautiful offering she'd made him. Her slim body had a wealth of inviting curves. He let his gaze touch on her breasts first, feeling a thrill of masculine pleasure when the nipples puckered and grew more rigid. His mouth watered, his fingers itching to touch and caress, but first he wanted to see all of her, every long, luscious inch. Reaching out, he caught hold of the sheet across her stomach and tugged it the rest of the way off her body, baring her thighs and long, lovely legs.

One tiny triangle of red silk kept him from seeing all of her. He wanted it gone. He heard Sallie's quick intake of breath when he grasped hold of the fabric.

"How fond are you of these panties?" he asked gruffly.

"Not... Not at all." she stuttered huskily.

With a twist and a tug, he snapped the fragile band that held the panties in place. Then he curled his fingers around the soft fabric that held the warmth of Sallie's body. He groaned as the feel generated even more heat in his veins. He wouldn't have thought it possible, but the sight of the dark, curling hair he'd uncovered made the ache in his loins grow fiercer.

"You're exquisite," he insisted roughly.

"No, I'm..." she started to argue, but her words turned into a hiss of surprise as he slid a hand between her thighs. Pleasure rippled through him as she parted her legs at his touch. He played with the tight curls for a few seconds and then dipped his fingers deeper, spreading, exploring, caressing.

Sallie's breathing grew noticeably rough. Her chest rose and fell more heavily with each breath. Her hands were knotted into fists at her sides and her legs shifted restlessly, but she didn't try to hinder his exploration. He found and pressed hard on the nub of nerves with his thumb while dipping two fingers into her moist heat, gently stretching the tightness. Her hips rose from the bed, arching closer to his touch.

"So responsive, so damned responsive," Cade ground out, fighting the need to sink himself so deeply into her that she'd never want another man. She was hot and wet and welcoming. He wanted her hard and fast, but, even more, he wanted to pleasure her beyond anything she'd ever imagined. He wanted to print himself indelibly on her flesh and her heart. A shudder racked him as he realized just how badly he wanted to lay claim to her, to take possession of more than her body.

"Cade!" Sallie cried out as he stroked her harder, pushing her higher and then still higher. She tried to grab him and drag him down to her, but he resisted. Once he was inside her, he'd lose control. He couldn't let that happen until he'd shown her how much she could enjoy their loving.

When touching her was no longer enough, he dropped to the bed on his knees, grasped her hips in his hands and lifted her to his mouth, caressing her with teeth and tongue and lips until he felt her whole body shuddering with climax. She screamed out her release, and he soaked up the sound, absorbing it into himself.

Now her body could more readily accept the invasion of his. While she still panted, he covered himself with one of the handful of condoms he'd collected from the bathroom, and then slid over her sweat-slick body. It tortured him to go slow when he desperately wanted fast and furious, but he forced himself to enter her with a long, gentle thrust. She stiffened a little and he gave her a few torturous minutes to adjust to his penetration. Her sheathing heat lit an answering inferno in him. Then he started moving again, in and out, in and out, he mentally choreographed the slow-motion movements to maintain his dwindling control.

Sallie climaxed a second time, her body tightening around him, her muscles milking him with unbearable pleasure. And Cade lost it. His body, too long denied, took on a mind of its own and began pounding into her with a fervor that wouldn't be denied. He grasped her head in his hands and sank his tongue into her mouth. When she greedily returned his kiss, he buried himself deep inside of her and came apart in her arms. An explosive release sent pleasure spiraling through him.

His arms trembled so much that he couldn't bear his own weight. Not wanting to crush her, he fell to her side, and then quickly disposed of the condom before collapsing again. For the next few minutes, they both lay still except for their heaving chests. Their ragged breathing was the only sound that broke the silence of the room. When Cade had recovered some of his strength, he turned to her again, planting his forearms on either side of her head and staring down into her beautifully flushed face.

"Sallie," he coaxed her to open her eyes. When her dark lashes swept upward, he almost melted. The look in them was sated, yet still deeply, heavily aroused.

"I'm sorry," he murmured, pressing a light kiss on her lips.

She tensed a little. "For what, exactly?"

"For forgetting the basic rules of seduction." He swept kisses over her cheeks and chin and mouth.

"I don't know anything about rules," she confessed breathily.

Cade nearly lost his train of thought when she brought her hands up to stroke his arms and shoulders. The heat of her touch singed him. Instead of cooling his desire, their lovemaking had intensified his need for her. Desire smoldered within him, making him hotter by the minute. He wanted to know the feel of her hands and mouth over every inch of his body, even though he was sure the pleasure would kill him.

"The first three rules are foreplay, foreplay, foreplay," he finally explained.

"We didn't do that?" she asked, her hands wandering to his backside to cup his buttocks.

Cade groaned, a deep, dark sound that rumbled from his chest as she squeezed his cheeks and seared his skin, branding him forever with her touch. The feel of her hands on him set his body aflame. How long had he secretly been hungering for the intimate contact?

"I kinda started at the finish line," he said, ashamed of his own juvenile impatience. "That's what usually happens in the back seat of a car."

"Really?"

The husky, sexily breathed question had him dipping his head and capturing her mouth again. He nibbled and licked and then thrust his tongue deeply into her softness. She thrilled him by letting her tongue slide sensuously along his and then sucking it strongly and impatiently. Her body quickened beneath him, and she dug her fingers deeper into his butt cheeks. The sting of her nails stirred a new erection to life, but he refused to be rushed this time.

"Foreplay," he muttered, determined to show her more than rutting desire. Sliding downward, he buried his face between her breasts, scattering kisses on the soft, dewy skin. It smelled of sophistication and sweetness, Sallie's unique scent. He wanted to taste her, so he let his tongue explore the curves of each breast. He lapped and laved and suckled her nipples until they stood at rigid attention. Then he plucked them with his fingers until her slender body drew tight and began to writhe against him. The low, keening moans she made slipped past his normal defenses and buried themselves deep in his heart. Her hands grew frantic as they caressed him, coaxing, tugging, urging him to hurry.

Instead, he slid further down her body and planted wet kisses across her ribs and abdomen. Her flesh quivered beneath his lips and he tried soothing it with the stroke of his tongue and the nip of his teeth. As his caresses slipped still lower, she squirmed and moaned and rocked her hips against him. She grasped his head with both hands, sinking her fingers into his hair as his mouth found its target.

Her body jerked, her fingers tightening painfully in his hair as he spread her legs and took his caresses even lower. When he sank his teeth into her feminine heat, she cried out in wild abandon, her body thrashing against the sheet. Her reaction pulsed through him in a rush of masculine triumph. This is what he wanted, what he'd yearned for so long—to make her wild with need. He wanted her screaming his name and begging for more. He desperately needed her to want him as he wanted her, to be a flame licking through her blood that couldn't be ignored or extinguished.

He drove her higher and higher, until she was nearing the peak again, but she twisted from his touch.

"Condom," she shouted on a harsh breath.

"Later," he argued.

"Now! I want you in me!"

Cade didn't make her ask twice. He sheathed himself and slid between her thighs, thrusting hard and deep. After the second stroke, she spiraled to a climax, but he was a long way from satisfaction. He drove her higher and higher, over and over again, giving her all the stimulation he could master. The next hour was spent teaching her how beautifully her body responded to his loving. He took his time, driving her slowly and then rapidly, and then slowly again until her incredible responsiveness drove him to find his own release.

Temporarily sated, Cade cradled Sallie in his arms. The room felt steamy from loving, the bed rumpled. Moonlight barely edged out total darkness. A perfect atmosphere for some serious pillow talk, and he really wanted to know more about his fabulous lover.

"So you've only been serious about one other man." It was a statement rather than a question. "Was that such a bad experience that you avoided other relationships or such an awesome one that you didn't think you could do better?"

"Definitely the former," she replied sleepily. "The experience was not a good one."

He heard reluctance to discuss the subject in her voice. She'd never shared much information about her personal life, but he wanted an intimacy with her that went beyond her sexy body. "Tell me about it," he coaxed softly.

"There's really not much to tell," she said and followed the words with a wide yawn.

"So it won't take long to share the details," he teased. "The sooner you explain, the sooner you get to sleep."

Sallie laughed softly. "That's blackmail, but I'm feeling really generous tonight."

"This morning," he corrected.

She nodded and grinned. "The other man was a young executive who worked for my father."

Cade uttered a low groan.

"Yeah," she agreed. "The same old, tired story. I thought we were madly in love, and he thought I was the key to my dad's kingdom."

"What happened to the shithead?"

She laughed out loud. "My dad booted him from the company, but he found another debutante to love. I hear he's doing well. I really don't care."

"No lingering yearning for him?"

"Nope. Not even a tiny craving."

"Good."

"Can I go to sleep now?"

Cade nodded, but he didn't think she saw or cared. She went out like a light. Sleep didn't come as easily to him. He thought about her father and the obscenely wealthy lifestyle she must have known. When it came to money and clout, he couldn't compete. What he had to do was prove how special he thought she was; as a woman, a lover, a partner. He'd never been one to think in terms of soulmates, but the more time they spent together, the more he believed she was his.

ಐఎಲ

Sallie woke just as dawn began to lighten the bedroom. Disoriented at first, the hard masculine arm across her waist alarmed her. Then she opened her eyes and saw Cade lying next to her. Her chest constricted, her heart began to pound, and her nerves sang with pleasure.

He had to be the most gorgeous man in the world. She'd often thought that, but now she knew it to be true. With his hair tousled and his body naked in the early morning light, he had a godlike beauty that put every other man she'd ever known to shame.

A tidal wave of doubt and insecurity washed over her. How could she hope to hold the attention of such a man? So many other women had tried and failed. Why should she imagine she'd be any different? What could she possibly offer him that he hadn't been offered so many times before?

Wasn't she just a passing fancy for him? Just an itch he needed to scratch? She'd promised herself an affair without emotional attachments, and yet she already found herself caring more than it was safe to care. Maybe Cade had made love to dozens of women the same way he'd made love to her, but that didn't make the experience any less new or awe inspiring. Was she already way out of her league?

As her gaze wandered down his chest to his waist, she watched in awe as his erection sprang to life. Her gaze darted back up to his face as he opened his eyes and gave her a slow, sexy grin.

"Good morning, beautiful," he said.

Sallie shoved the negative thoughts from her mind, determined to enjoy every minute of his flirtation. "I'm not beautiful," she argued softly.

Cade's brows creased in a frown. He slipped an arm beneath her and pulled her close to his warm body. She molded her curves to his.

"I think you have the most beautiful eyes I've ever seen," he told her, looking deeply into those same eyes. "Your skin is so soft and so smooth." He stroked his thumb across her cheek. "Your lips are full and generous, your mouth, perfect." He dipped his head to give her a kiss.

Sallie thrilled at the light caress and the sincerity of his tone. He seemed to appreciate her best features, helping her feel beautiful and confident in a way she'd never expected. Snuggling closer, she slipped her hand around his waist to stroke the hard, firm flesh of his backside.

Cade moaned softly, assuring her that he welcomed her touch.

"I hope I already convinced you how much I admire the rest of your body," he murmured before nuzzling her ear.

"I admire your body, too," she teased, nibbling his chin. A huge understatement since they'd spent the entire night worshiping each other's bodies.

"Wanna make love again?"

"I'll have to think about it."

"Think about it up here," he replied, pulling her over his body.

Sallie didn't resist the invitation. She reached toward his dwindling pile of condoms and slowly covered his erection, caressing him to rigidity in the process. He started mumbling encouragement, but soon began to rock his hips in impatient demand to join their bodies. She widened her thighs to straddle his hips, and then slowly impaled herself on his rigid flesh. After that, they moved together in perfect harmony, reaching for and finding complete satisfaction.

Spent, but content, she fell asleep in Cade's arms.

The next time she woke, she was alone in bed with the covers drawn over her. She heard the shower running and knew it was well past time to be out of bed. Smiling at her uncharacteristically self-indulgent behavior, she gradually stretched the kinks out of her body.

Despite getting very little sleep, she felt fabulous. A little sore in spots, but certainly well-loved. She'd always wondered if Cade would be a selfish lover, but he'd certainly put that thought to rest last night. He'd been demanding and insatiable, yet he gave much more than he took. She didn't think there was an inch of her body that he hadn't explored with his hands or hot, wet, adoring mouth.

Whew! Just thinking about the intimacies they'd shared brought a blush to her cheeks. She'd read about some of the things he'd shown her, but she'd certainly never experienced the majority of them. Sallie wondered if he'd be shocked to know that she wanted to join him in the shower, wanted to see the water sluicing over his sleek, muscular frame. Would he draw the line at that kind of sharing or would he welcome her with his hard, hungry body?

Before she could put the questions to a test, she

heard the water shut off in the bathroom and heaved a deep sigh. Then she looked toward the doorway and smiled with pleasure as Cade appeared. He had one towel draped around his waist and used another to dry his hair. When their gazes met, he gave her an incredibly warm, sweet smile.

"Sorry if the shower woke you," he said. "This downstairs one rattles a lot."

"It didn't bother me," she replied, and then boldly shared her earlier thought with him. "I was more bothered by the prospect of joining you."

Surprise widened his eyes, and then speculation. "You're pulling my leg," he accused. "You weren't really considering it."

"I might have been," she taunted flirtatiously, pulling the sheet to her chin.

Cade tossed aside both towels and made a running dive to the bed. Sallie squealed as he caught her in his arms and wrestled his way under the covers. She briefly fended him off but was soon wrapping her arms around him, drawing him closer and succumbing to his kisses.

"You're all wet," she finally said when she could catch her breath again.

"Wet and wanting you," he added, rocking his hips against hers. "If you don't make a run for the bathroom soon, I'll have to ravish your body again."

"Maybe we could make the run together." She'd see if he was serious about sharing another level of intimacy.

She had her answer in an instant. Cade tightened his

hold on her and lifted her from the bed. She clung to him as he strode toward the bathroom, and then they shared both a shower and their bodies again.

༄༅༄༅

Later in the day, they sat on the front porch swing, lazily enjoying a light afternoon breeze. Sallie rested her head on Cade's shoulder as they discussed some of the ranch's operations. He'd shown her around the property and introduced her to several of the ranch hands. She'd had lots of questions and he'd patiently answered them all. His pride in his family home had never been more evident. She wondered how he could stand to live in the city when he so obviously thrived in the wide, open space of the ranch.

"Why do you ever leave it?" she asked.

Cade hesitated, and Sallie wondered if he'd refuse to answer. Maybe it was a really sensitive subject for him. She'd never given it much thought, she had always supposed he loved the city life.

"The ranch has always belonged to Trey," he finally explained. "We share the inheritance equally, but he's always been the caretaker of the property. In my younger days, I was too restless to settle down to the day-to-day routine of it. I had a passion for tackling the corporate world and testing the designs I'd been developing since I was old enough to understand what makes things tick."

"That's why you studied engineering?"

"It came naturally to me."

She understood because she had the same natural affinity for business. "These last couple years, I've noticed you spending more and more time here in New Mexico. Do you ever think you'll tire of the corporate rat race?"

"Life on the ranch is a lot simpler, more physically demanding, but equally rewarding. Not better, but different. More permanent. Does that make sense?"

She nodded against his shoulder. The ranch would always be home for him and his roots were deeply buried in the land.

"I'd like to have my own house out here one of these days and a section of the ranch to run, but first I have to make sure there'll always be enough money to protect the land. We almost lost it when Mom and Dad died. I have to make sure Langden Industries can be depended on in the lean years."

Sallie had always considered Cade a driven man, but she'd never really understood what drove him. She'd thought he was too much like her father in that respect. Her dad couldn't stand to be outdone by anyone. He saw every challenge as a test of his executive prowess, and he hated being bested by anyone. It was a matter of personal pride to him. For Cade, apparently, the need to succeed had a far deeper meaning. Maybe she'd been judging him unfairly all these years.

"You're committed to preserving this part of our American Heritage," she said, her tone letting him know that she found that admirable.

"That I am," he answered, dropping a kiss on her forehead. "I want generations of Langdens to have the same opportunities my ancestors gave me. Whether or not they choose to live on the land will be up to them, but Trey and I made a pact to protect it with every ounce of our strength."

"Which is considerable."

"Which is considerable," he agreed.

They shared a smile.

"What about you, Miss Very-Smart-Rich-Girl?" he asked, his brow furrowing. "Did you really finish college by the age of nineteen?"

"I did, but you have to remember that I had an army of tutors. Since all my other activities were severely limited, I spent more than the usual amount of time studying."

"Ugh."

"Yeah."

"What can you possibly want that you haven't already had or couldn't buy for yourself? Your financial future has to be as secure as it gets."

As heiress to the Harriman billions, she'd never have to worry about money. That was fact. But would he scoff if she told him the truth? That being a normal, wage-earning citizen made her happy. That she wanted the same thing the majority of other women wanted—a home, a husband who adored her, a couple of children. She wanted the freedom to live her life as she saw fit without the constant threat to her safety or the notoriety that came with the financial security.

"I want a future without armed bodyguards," she said.

His hold on her tightened. "We'll get this guy soon and you won't have to be afraid anymore. You're safe here."

She felt totally safe in Cade's arms, but worried about putting him at risk. "I know, yet it seems there's always someone else who's lazy enough or greedy enough to prey on others. They killed my brother without hesitation. He was just a commodity to them. Dad planned to pay the ransom as soon as he had evidence that Brent was still alive, but the kidnappers couldn't provide it. They stopped communicating with Mother and Dad. Brent's body turned up a few weeks later. Those were the longest weeks of my life."

"They never identified the kidnappers?"

"No, even though my dad put all his considerable power and tons of money into the investigation."

"I can't imagine that kind of loss or that kind of frustration," Cade said quietly. "Trey, Jillian and Eli are all the family I have. I'd do everything in my power to protect them."

"My dad felt the same way. That's why I became a prisoner in our home. He and Mother were paranoid about my safety. I understood, yet I nearly went crazy with the restrictions and security."

"You were just a teenager then? A little rebellious? Is that when you fell in love with the slimeball you mentioned last night?"

Sallie thought about her one truly rebellious act as a

teenager. She'd run away from home with a man who'd promised her love and marriage. When he'd pressed her for premarital sex, she'd gotten cold feet. He'd been furious and forced himself on her. Fortunately, he hadn't been brutal, just overpowering. He could have faced charges, but she'd been too guilty and ashamed to tell anyone. She'd called her parents and gone home without telling them any details. Nowadays she wondered how many other young women's trust had been violated in the same fashion.

Her big escape plan had been a disaster, but it had taught her a hard lesson. The memory still had the power to humiliate her. She might never be able to share all the sordid details.

"Yes, he was involved in my only rebellious act, but it convinced my parents of how badly I wanted a life outside the mansion gates. That's why they helped me establish a new identity."

Cade went quiet for a few minutes. "I don't suppose you're going to tell me his name?"

She shook her head. "Nope."

"You have a real cruel streak, woman," he accused, pulling her more tightly against his chest.

Sallie laughed softly and gave him an unrepentant grin. In response, he pulled her onto his lap. She wrapped her arms around his neck, and he brought his mouth down to hers and kissed her deeply. She welcomed the thrust of his tongue, using hers to return the caresses.

"I have a confession," he told her when he lifted his

head again.

She felt the brush of his breath against the dampness of her lips. "I love confessions," she whispered, flicking her tongue out to paint his mouth.

Cade moaned softly and tightened his hold on her. "I've spent the whole day playing polite host when all I really wanted was you back in my bed."

She feigned a shocked expression. "That's horrible."

"I'm dying," he countered, rubbing his erection against her hip, showing her how much he wanted her again.

"It's not bedtime yet," she teased.

"We could watch the sunset from the bedroom," he suggested, nibbling on her lips.

He slid one hand between them and cupped her breast, strumming his thumb across the nipple until it puckered. She felt the caress deep in the pit of her stomach, his touch making her damp and achy.

"Or we could try having sex right here on the swing," he said before deepening the kiss into a tongue-lashing, erotic invitation.

She squirmed restlessly. On her next breath, she begged, "Bedroom!"

"Your wish is my command," he said, rising and lifting her with him.

Sallie clung tightly as they made their way into the house. She delighted in Cade's desire for her. She didn't know how long it would last, but she'd promised herself to enjoy every minute. Tomorrow could take care of itself.

Within a few minutes, they had tumbled into bed and stripped each other of clothing. Skin-to-skin and heart-to-heart, they made love with an intensity that left them both shuddering in release. Then they lay in each other's arms and watched the sunset from the bedroom window.

When their bodies had cooled and their breathing had settled, Cade gently stroked the hair from her face and returned to his early questions.

"You never told me what you want from the future," he said. "Besides being free from bodyguards."

Sallie wondered, yet again, what he would think of the truth. How many times had he heard it from other women? Would it send him running? She decided to offer it, in part. "Just a normal life with a normal family."

"Just a husband, kids, a dog?" he asked. "No high-profile executive career? You don't want to step into your father's shoes one of these days?"

She listened to his low tone, but didn't hear any mockery. He almost sounded wistful. "I'm as high-profile as I care to be. I've already made that clear to my dad."

"And he hasn't tried to change your mind?"

"Of course he has," she said, smoothing a hand over his cheek. Her fingers tingled when she brushed the stubble of new whiskers. "He wouldn't be the powerhouse he is without giving it his best efforts. I'm just not interested."

"I guess I never pegged you for the home and hearth type," said Cade.

"Why?"

"Nothing about your current lifestyle or what I've learned about your background suggests that you'd be content with the norm."

"Yes, it does, really," she argued. "I've lived a very ordinary life these past few years, and I was content with it until some psycho started giving me grief."

"Content, but were you happy?"

"Money can't buy happiness, Cade. That much I learned at a very early age. True happiness comes from the people in our lives and the relationships we nurture. I have no doubt that I want a normal life with normal relationships. All the rest is just icing on the cake."

Cade took her hand in his and brought it to his mouth. He kissed the palm and then each finger. "I find that very, very interesting."

Sallie liked the idea of destroying his preconceived ideas about her. She wanted him to find her interesting and unpredictable. She didn't mention that she also wanted the normal man in her life to adore her beyond all measure, but she supposed that really was more fairy tale than practical.

All thoughts went by the wayside when he spread kisses to her wrist and then up her arm. Before long, they were lost again in passion.

Chapter Nine

The next day dawned clear and bright. Cade and Sallie slept late, made love, and then slept again. They didn't finish breakfast until nearly noon. While they tidied the kitchen, they heard the sound of a helicopter approaching.

"We don't get many 'copters passing by," said Cade, his brows creasing in a frown. "We're too far off the beaten path."

They listened as the hum of the helicopter rotors grew steadily louder. "It sounds like it's right over us," added Sallie.

Just then, the intercom beeped and the ranch foreman's voice greeted them. "Cade, looks like that helo is going to set down in the field west of the house. You expecting company?"

"No," his tone was terse. "How about you get together a few men and bring 'em up here."

"Will do." The connection was abruptly broken.

Sallie didn't like the sound of the exchange or the sudden tension in Cade's body.

"What's happening?"

"I don't know," he said grimly. "Since we're not expecting anyone by air, we'd best prepare for trouble."

He led her back into his bedroom where French doors faced the field in question. They had a clear view of the helicopter coming in to land.

A heavy sigh escaped Sallie as she recognized the familiar black and orange of her father's fleet of aircraft. "You can call off your men. It's one of my dad's."

"You're sure?"

"I'm sure."

"But we don't know that he sent it. Somebody might have hijacked it."

She hadn't thought of that, but her mind wasn't really geared toward danger or threats to her personal safety. "I'll have to wait and see who's aboard."

"Your mom and dad?" Cade had been ready to load his rifle, but he set it aside and slipped an arm around her waist. "Do you think they found out their baby girl is spending time alone with a man and they've come to rescue you?"

Sallie laughed softly at his teasing, preferring it to the tension he'd been exhibiting minutes ago. "Not very likely. My mother thinks helicopters are a totally uncivilized form of transportation, and they always give my dad headaches." She didn't mention that her parents despaired about the lack of prospective mates in her life.

As they watched the 'copter stir up dust a couple

hundred yards from the patio off Cade's bedroom, Sallie slid closer to him. Intuition warned her that their privacy and the intimacy it had afforded them would soon be destroyed. She pressed her back against his chest, and he locked his arms protectively around her waist. Resting her hands on his, they waited.

Once the rotors of the aircraft had come to a stop, a single man alighted from the machine. He walked slowly, steadily, confidently across the grassy field toward the house. By the time he had moved within a few yards of the patio, several of the ranch hands had also rounded the house and set up a human barrier.

"It's Alec. Alec Walker," Sallie told Cade. "My dad's right-hand man."

The man in question stood nearly six feet tall, had broad shoulders and a lean body. His inky black hair was cut in a severely conservative style. Despite the heat of the day and his mode of transportation, he wore a three-piece suit, a white shirt and a tie.

Cade grunted. "A buttoned-up, totally dedicated executive, I'd say."

"That he is," agreed Sallie, her tone and body growing tenser. "And my dad respects that. He's definitely not an errand boy. Walker wouldn't be here unless there's a serious problem."

"You're sure he can be trusted?"

"As sure as I can be about anything these days. If they'd had a falling out, my mother would have let me know immediately. She thinks Alec is a workaholic stuffed-shirt whose exemplary executive skills keep my dad inspired to work too hard."

"So what do you think brings superman to my humble abode?"

"Me, I suppose." She squeezed his hands, and his arms tightened around her. She loved the feel of his warmth and hardness, loved being so close to him, and dreaded the end of their time together. "I made my dad a promise when he helped me buy a new identity."

"What kind of promise?"

"That any time he felt my safety was threatened, I'd come home on his request."

"You think he's learned about your stalker and sent his assistant to fetch you?"

"That would be my guess."

Sallie felt Cade's chest heave in a deep sigh. Her chest rose and fell in the same rhythm.

"Then I suppose we'd better find out for sure."

Walker halted near the edge of the patio. He nodded to the men gathered there, and told them he had business with Sallie. Cade withdrew his arms from her waist and opened the sliding doors. He stepped onto the patio with her following closely, yet shielded by his body. Sallie's gaze met that of her dad's assistant.

"Hello, Alec," she said, stepping around Cade, but slipping into her earlier position with her back against his chest. His arms immediately enveloped her.

Walker nodded his head in greeting. "Sallie."

"What brings you to the wilds of New Mexico?" she asked. "Are my parents okay?"

"They're both fine, but worried. Your dad sent me to collect you."

"He knows I won't climb aboard a helicopter with anyone. Not even you," she added, flashing him a serene smile.

"He didn't expect you to be too cooperative." The executive's stern expression cracked in a wry smile. "He told me to tell you he had a yellow ribbon tied around a tree for you."

Sallie tipped her head and whispered to Cade. "That's my dad's latest security code," she explained.

Cade didn't seem impressed. "And you're sure nobody could coerce it from him?"

"Not likely," she directed her gaze back to her dad's envoy. "Dad has a series of codes that I need before I trust anyone. I'm the only one who knows about the series. Mother doesn't even know them."

Since Sallie had inherited her dad's gift with numbers, they'd often played number games when she lived at home. Now she waited for Walker to give her the right sequence of prime numbers. When he'd completed the ten-number series, she sighed and turned to Cade again.

Speaking quietly so only he could hear her, she said. "My parents would die before compromising my safety. If Dad had given the sequence in a reverse order, it would be a warning of trouble. It's not, so I have to go with him," she explained. "I promised."

Their gazes met for a long minute. "I can take you wherever you need to go."

"I gave him my word that I would come whenever and however he asked. The fact that he sent Walker is proof of his concern. He's kept his end of the bargain for five years. I can't change the rules now."

"Then we both go."

Sallie gave him a smile. "You don't have to do that." They'd only been lovers for a couple days. It was all uncharted territory for her, and she had no way of knowing how important their new physical relationship was to Cade. She didn't want him going with her because of some misguided sense of chivalry.

His gaze stayed focused on her face. "Would it make you uncomfortable to introduce me to your parents?"

Surprise had her shaking her head. "No, not at all, but I don't want you to feel obligated in any way."

"Obligated?" he seemed to consider her choice of words. "I swear I don't feel the least bit obligated. Where are we going?"

"Why don't you send your men back to work and we'll talk to Alec?"

Cade nodded in agreement, turned and nodded to his foreman. The ranch hands gradually dispersed, tipping their hats to Sallie as they disappeared around the house again. Alec stepped onto the patio and she directed him toward the door that lead into the kitchen rather than the bedroom.

Sallie introduced the two men and they shook hands. "Does your pilot want to come down and have some coffee or something before we leave again?" she asked, making it clear that she planned to accompany him when he left.

"He said he's fine. He has a thermos in the chopper."

"Exactly where are we going?"

"Your parents are at their place in Phoenix," explained Walker. "I have the Lear in Albuquerque, so the flight won't take us too long from there."

"Cade's going with us," she said.

He nodded, showing no expression.

Cade leaned against the doorframe, his arms crossed. "Mind telling me how you managed to track Sallie down?"

Alec appeared to choose his words carefully. "Mr. Harriman likes to know where to reach her at all times."

That snapped Sallie to attention. "My dad is having me watched?" she asked, her tone terse.

"I'm not touching that one," said the other man. "You'll have to discuss it with your father."

Her response was an indignant growl. "There's some coffee left in the pot," she said, remembering he was a caffeine addict. "Help yourself. Cade and I have to pack."

༒༒༒

By late afternoon they'd entered her parents' high-security compound in Phoenix with its relatively modest-looking pink-stucco home. Sallie felt tired and grubby but she looked forward, as always, to seeing her mother and dad. Due to hectic schedules, they didn't get a chance to visit very often. She loved them dearly, even though she had no desire to live in their social sphere.

She'd inherited her height from both of them. The Harrimans, Carlton and Lynette, were tall and slender with deeply tanned skin and silvery hair. Sallie had inherited her mother's oval-shaped face and her father's gray-green eyes. Her father always looked distinguished and her mother elegant. They were casually dressed yet it didn't detract from the overall air of sophistication and wealth.

Sallie hugged her mother first and then got a bear hug from her dad. They all started talking and laughing at once, an open and obvious display of their love.

"How was your flight?" asked her mother.

"Long and boring."

"You always say that," her dad chided.

"Because I hate flying," she shot back. "Although Cade's company helped to make this one a little less annoying." With that, she turned to Cade and properly introduced him to her parents. They all shook hands and exchanged greetings.

"You're both okay?" Sallie asked next. She'd worried the whole trip that one of them had serious health issues.

"We're fine." Carlton quickly reassured her. "That's not why I had Alec come get you. But let's not tackle that discussion until you've had time to rest."

Sallie sighed. "I am really beat. Is it okay to crash a

while?"

"Certainly!" Lynette quickly took over hostess duties. "I've had a room freshened for Mr. Langden..."

"Cade, please," he insisted, winning himself a smile from her mother.

Then she turned to Sallie. "Please show Cade to the room on the opposite side of the hall from yours. Dinner won't be for another couple of hours, so take your time and relax. We can catch up with news once you've rested."

Sallie gave her mother another peck on the cheek. "Sounds good."

She and Cade started gathering up their suitcases.

Carlton offered to help, but they assured him it wasn't necessary. He nodded and told them, "Janet is the only fulltime staff we have here but she'll be happy to get you anything you'd like. Just use the intercom in your rooms if you'd like anything from the kitchen."

Sallie glanced at Cade, but he shook his head. "I think we're fine for now. Just a shower and a nap," she said, and then felt herself blushing as she remembered the shower she'd shared with him yesterday. One glance at her telltale expression had him nudging her along the hallway.

"Our rooms are on the left side of the house," Sallie explained, keeping her voice conversational even though she had an uncharacteristic urge to giggle. She gave one last wave to her parents and turned down the hall toward the bedrooms. The house had four guest suites, but she'd laid claim to one of them. Her parents' suite of rooms was on the opposite side of the house, allowing Cade and her a little privacy.

"They're the last two rooms on this side of the house," Sallie explained, pointing toward the doors at the end of the hall. "Mine's on the right, yours is on the left, and we both have great views of the setting sun. If I weren't so exhausted, I'd play the good hostess, but I'm going to let you fend for yourself."

"I think I can manage," he said, stepping into her room to drop off her largest case. "Any chance we share a bathroom?"

Sallie laughed softly. "In a Carlton Harriman home? You must be kidding. Only the best for his guests. We each have our own bedroom, sitting room and spa-bath."

"Too bad," said Cade, dropping a kiss on her nose. "I like sharing."

Sallie dropped her purse and the small bag she was carrying. She lifted her arms and was swiftly drawn into his embrace. They hugged tightly and laid their heads together, but both were too tired to do much else.

"Rest," she said, finally withdrawing from his arms. "I'm going to crash for an hour or so and then soak in the tub. I'll come knocking at your door when it's time for dinner."

Cade nodded, picked his case back up and moved across the hall to his room. She gave him a weary smile, closed her door and then threw herself across the bed and fell asleep within minutes.

Sallie kept a small wardrobe of designer clothes at her parents' house. She'd only packed casual clothes for the ranch, but she wanted to wear something ultra-feminine this evening. She chose an emerald green gown with a scooped neckline and cap sleeves. The fabric was soft and clingy, the design understated. It had been created to accent a woman's figure and that's exactly what it did. The neckline draped just low enough to reveal a tantalizing amount of cleavage. The tight bodice plumped her breasts and left no room for a bra. Deep tucks at the waistline made the rest of her figure look round and full.

The gown's hem fell to her calves, but had slits on either side that bared her legs up to mid-thigh. She hoped the total effect would drive Cade crazy with desire. Just the thought of it had her nipples pouting against the fabric and sending a sizzle of excitement over the rest of her. It had been less than twelve hours since they'd last made love and she was already craving his touch. A lot.

Deciding not to dwell on her growing addiction to Cade's loving, she concentrated on the finishing touches of makeup and hair. A chignon of loose curls topped her head with little wispy curls tickling her neck and nape. Her thoughts drifted to her lover again. She knew he preferred her hair down but she hoped this different style would capture his imagination.

Once satisfied that she'd done all she could do, she dabbed perfume on her wrists and headed for his room. At her knock, the door swung open and she caught her breath. She'd gotten so used to Cade in his boots and jeans that his appearance took her by surprise. He hadn't put on anything too formal, but the khaki pants and light yellow polo shirt highlighted his deep tan, his broad chest and lean hips. He looked every inch the sexy hunk she knew him to be.

The slow perusal he made of her had her heart skipping a beat, and then another.

"H-e-l-l-o, gorgeous," he drawled in a low, sexy tone. Then he reached for her, sliding both hands around her waist and pulling her close. He nibbled on her neck and whispered in her ear. "Wanna make love?"

Her body answered his question with a resounding "Yes!" but she tried to keep her voice calm and level. It wouldn't do for him to know just how badly she wanted to get him naked. "Dinner in a few minutes," she reminded him.

"A few minutes won't get it," he swore gruffly. "I want lots and lots of time."

His words and tone sent a quiver of longing over her. Damn, she had it bad. He had her caught in a web of desire so complex, yet so basic that it amazed her. It felt as natural and comfortable as breathing, but totally unique in her experience.

"Think your folks will come looking for us if we don't show to eat?"

She pulled back slightly and pressed a kiss on his nose. "They'd never be so rude, but I'd rather not face them an hour late and looking like a wanton."

Cade cupped her hips with his hands, reluctant to let go of her. "Do I make you feel wanton?" he asked, his tone suggesting that her answer held great importance to him. Before she could answer, his grip tightened on her hips and his tone went gruff. "I hope so, because you make me feel savage and possessive."

She stared deeply into his eyes, amazed by his sudden vehemence. "You're not the savage, possessive type," she reminded him softly.

He made a rough sound and slowly released her, turning toward the hallway. He slid a guiding arm around her waist and visibly relaxed. "You're teaching me all sorts of new things about myself," he added in his normal easy tone.

Sallie didn't comment but she silently admitted the same about him. He'd introduced her to a whole new realm of emotions and physical pleasure. She'd convinced herself that she should indulge in the physical side of their relationship but she was still really wary of the emotional aspects. As they walked toward the dining room, their bodies brushed against each other in perfect rhythm. She felt a unique contentment. Two halves to a whole, she thought, knowing that it was very emotionally risky to think that way.

She'd never been a risk taker.

Conversation at dinner was exactly what Sallie expected. They started with general comments about the weather and world affairs as they ate. By dessert, her parents had begun a polite interrogation of Cade. She imagined they'd already had him thoroughly investigated, but he obligingly supplied details about his upbringing, his schooling and his family. Sallie was surprised but pleased that he made no effort to charm them. Instead of the polite social manner she was used to, he offered them more genuine insight to his life and personality. He shared childhood stories about growing up on the ranch and always trying to emulate his big brother. With a little more prodding, he discussed his deceased parents and how losing them had affected his life. She learned things she'd never known, things that endeared him to her even more.

She could almost sense the moment her parents gave Cade their silent approval. They might not like the idea of her having a lover, but they approved of her choice. It gave her a warm glow of happiness to know that they liked him in his most natural self.

By the coffee stage, her parents turned their full attention to her. Even though they spoke regularly on the phone, they always had an unending amount of questions. They wanted to know everything she'd been doing since they'd last seen her. They wanted updates and details on her day-to-day life, her work, her friends, and everything else about her life.

Sallie knew the routine and normally didn't mind answering all their questions. She'd never doubted her parents' love and devotion. As their only surviving child, she felt a strong need to make them proud and nurture a close relationship. The tricky part was giving them details about recent weeks without mentioning the weird stuff.

Cade helped her when the questions hedged too close to areas she didn't want to discuss. He smoothly changed the subject when she seemed at a loss. Every time he intervened to help, she gave him a warm smile. He returned each one with more warmth, his expression assuring her that she could depend on him for support. After a while, it grew increasingly difficult to focus on the conversation and not the man who'd captured her attention. Her gaze locked with his and she kept getting lost in the warmth of his beautiful eyes.

When Lynette gently cleared her throat, Sallie realized that she and Cade had been absorbed with each other to the point of forgetting they weren't alone. Having no idea how long they'd been staring at each other in fascinated silence, she dragged her gaze from him and gave her mother an apologetic smile.

"Is it time to vacate the dining room so Janet can clean up?" she asked, neatly folding her napkin and placing it on the table.

Her mother did the same. "If you're sure you don't want anything else to eat."

Everyone assured her they'd had plenty. When Sallie started to rise, Cade moved to hold her chair, managing to brush a soft kiss across her neck in the process. The old fashioned courtesy combined with his sexy attention made her knees go weak. Having Cade's worldly charm directed solely on her made her feel incredibly special. She kept reminding herself not to take it too seriously. He'd charmed more than his fair share of women and she needed to keep reminding herself of that fact. He just had a knack for making women feel unique and desirable.

"Why don't we go to the library and have a glass of brandy?" asked Carlton. He put a hand at his wife's waist and led the way.

She and Cade followed her parents.

The library was Sallie's favorite room of the house. The dark wood paneling and southwest décor made it cozy and appealing. The furniture was a collection of buttery yellow leather. She sat down on the loveseat and Cade settled close to her side.

Lynette took a seat on the sofa while Carlton poured them each a snifter of brandy. When he sat down beside her mother, a sudden tension filled the room. Sallie knew her dad was finally getting around to telling her why he'd sent Walker after her.

"I'm afraid I have some bad news," he began.

"And a confession," added Lynette.

Sallie could tell that her dad was having a hard time finding the words to explain why he'd panicked about her safety. For a man who conversed with dignitaries all over the world, his reluctance was alarming. Tension began to sing through her body. Whatever he had to confess, she knew she wasn't going to like it.

"I'm afraid I haven't been completely honest with you these past few years," he told her, staring into his drink. "When your mother and I agreed to help you create a new identity, we promised to bow out and let you live a normal life."

Sallie glanced from one to the other. "You've done

that."

"Not exactly, dear," offered Lynette. "We couldn't bear to let you live without protection." Her eyes beseeched her daughter to understand.

"I decided to let part of my security team keep a watch over you," confessed Carlton, pushing out the words in a rush. "They've been guarding you all these years."

Sallie watched the myriad of expressions cross her parents' faces and grew tenser. "Guarding?"

"My security team has been keeping a 24/7 watch on you," Carlton admitted. "Just like they did when you lived at home, but without being so conspicuous."

Sallie tried to absorb the full meaning of his confession. "You've been spying on me for five years? Watching my every move all this time?" she asked in disbelief.

"Not spying," Lynette quickly interjected. "I promise you that we didn't have anyone watching you and reporting back to us about your day-to-day routine."

"The security staff was supposed to keep a general watch on your home and workplace," explained her father. "They were never supposed to invade your privacy, and they only reported to me if they thought you might be in danger."

"You had me watched around the clock and you don't call that an invasion of privacy?" she demanded, growing more agitated with every word.

A wild mixture of emotions swirled through her. She tipped back her glass, drained the brandy and slammed the snifter onto the coffee table. How could she not have noticed that kind of constant surveillance? The thought of it made her feel stupid and humiliated and furious. She wanted to stomp her feet and scream at the injustice of it, but she clung to her control. She wouldn't behave like the schoolgirl they thought needed protecting.

Cade slipped an arm around her shoulders, and his support calmed her a little. If he'd had any doubt about her poor little rich girl story, at least he'd have a better understanding now.

"All the security detail did was report to us that you were safe and you weren't associating with anyone with a criminal background," said her dad. "We didn't pay them to pry into your personal life. We just hired them to police your neighborhood and watch for unexpected threats."

Sallie felt Cade's arm tighten around her and a new tension in his body. "So you know about the recent problems?" he asked.

She shot a glance at him and then at her father. If he'd been paying for her protection, where the hell had his men been while she'd been harassed these past few weeks?

"We know part of it," said Carlton.

"You knew about Sallie's stalker?" asked Cade, his tone grim. "And you didn't alert us?"

Carlton tossed back the contents of his glass and set it next to Sallie's on the table. Her whole body stiffened as she waited for the rest of the story. Her dad looked directly at her.

"Do you remember Harold Carmichael?"

Sallie thought about it for a minute. "Of course, he was one of the security team when we lived in New York."

Carlton nodded. "He kept your mother and me sane when your brother disappeared. I don't know how we would have handled it without his support. Then he was instrumental in finding Brent's body."

Even after all these years, the words were as hard for her to hear as they appeared to be hard for her father to say. The old, familiar wave of pain washed over her along with the memories of long, dark days when their lives were a nightmare of frenzied media attention and the misery of deep, aching loss.

"I remember. You made him my personal bodyguard after that. He insisted I take self-defense lessons and learn to fire a handgun."

"Right. We trusted him more than anyone on the team. That's why we asked him to continue your security when you moved to Dallas. He's been in charge of your personal detail every since."

"All these years?" groused Sallie, embarrassed by the very thought. "He must have been bored out of his mind." She didn't mention that he also must have been very good at subterfuge if she never noticed his existence. "What an absolute waste of time and money!"

Lynette looked directly at her. "It gets worse," she admitted gruffly.

Chapter Ten

Sallie couldn't imagine anything much worse, but she looked to her dad for an explanation.

"Harold generally checks in with me once a month, just to let me know that everything is okay," said Carlton.

"But you haven't heard from him in a while, have you?" asked Cade. The two men exchanged knowing glances.

"No, and all my efforts to contact him have been fruitless. I finally heard some disturbing information from another man on his team. It seems that Harold has gone rogue on us. He's developed an unhealthy fixation on Sallie. A few months ago, he fired most of the other men who've been working with him."

"Months? How could you not know? Aren't you paying their salaries?" asked Sallie.

"He's pretty slick and he knows a lot about my business. He also knew some of the long-time staff. He created fake identities and apparently I've been paying a phantom team for the past six months or so. When the dead body of one of those men was discovered in Dallas, Alec got suspicious. He put my current security staff to work and they discovered that Carmichael had gone off the deep end."

Sallie's stomach rolled at the lengths the bodyguard had gone to dupe her dad. She knew it had to be making him both furious and sick with self-disgust, but that didn't make her any more forgiving. Her dad was actually financing a man to harass her and Cade. A man who might be capable of murder. Not to mention the damage he'd done to Langdens'.

"Ohmigod!" Sallie turned to Cade with a sudden thought. "The man in the service vehicle at my house! The one who changed my tire. That was him. Carmichael. He's a short, stocky man. He's put on some weight in the past few years, but now that Dad reminded me, I'm almost sure. I was never allowed to go anywhere without him back then. Ohmigod! How could I not have recognized him at the time?"

A shudder of revulsion coursed through her. He'd been close enough to touch her. It was one thing to know she had a stalker, but even worse to know that the stalker had intimate knowledge of her family and her whole life. That he'd been trusted with her family's lives.

Cade gathered her close and pressed her head against his shoulder. Sallie slipped her arms around his waist and accepted the comfort of his arms. Another chill raced over her at the thought of all those spooky phone calls, the messages that seemed so intimately familiar. Now that the caller had been identified, it was even creepier.

"You think that this man, Carmichael, killed one of

his cohorts?"

Cade's question reminded Sallie of the tall, thin man they'd seen at the tavern. He must have been involved with Carmichael's scheme in some fashion.

Carlton rose from his seat, refilled everyone's snifters, and then slowly answered. "Roy Winerman was one of the men on my payroll and apparently the only one still working with Carmichael. We think he was willing to go along with him to a point, but then got cold feet when Carmichael started losing touch with reality.

"Roy made a few calls to my office and left cryptic messages," said Carlton. "Then he stopped calling and seemed to drop off the end of the earth. When we tried to track him down, we learned he'd been killed by a hit-and-run driver in Dallas. The police there didn't have any reason to suspect a deliberate murder, so they didn't investigate any further. We can't be sure what happened."

"Where's Carmichael now?" asked Cade.

"The Dallas police have an all-points bulletin out for him and expect to make an arrest soon. They've been keeping a close watch at his apartment and Sallie's condo. They figure he'll show up sooner or later, and that he's too obsessed with Sallie to stay in hiding very long. As soon as they have him in custody, I'll send my top security men to Texas."

Sallie shuddered at being the object of anyone's maniacal obsession, especially a man she'd known and trusted. Cade's arm tightened around her. "Do you think he had anything to do with Brent's kidnapping?" she asked.

Her dad slipped his arm around her mother who was visibly shaken by the suggestion. "We're checking into it. We had so few clues at the time and so little physical evidence that we'll probably never be certain. Unless he confesses. But it's beginning to look like he might have been involved in some capacity."

Sallie's stomach rolled at the thought. How sick would a man have to be to kidnap and murder a child and then continue to play the role of protector for the family? How could he have faced them every day, watching them grieve while knowing his own part in the heinous crime? To accept a salary from the family he'd betrayed so horribly? She shook her head to rid it of the painful, unanswerable questions.

"What now?"

Her father responded. "We hoped you'd stay here until we know Carmichael is in custody."

"That could be weeks or months," she protested. "He's proven that he's smart and devious. Look how long he's gotten away with kidnapping and murder. It's not going to be easy to find him."

"As soon as there's some word from the Dallas Police Department, I'll send Alec out there. I trust him with my life and yours. He'll keep us apprised of the situation. He's assured me that the Dallas PD has been very cooperative and he's checking in with them regularly."

"We still can't hide out indefinitely," said Sallie. She risked a glance at Cade, wondering if he thought she was the worst lover he'd ever known. Lately, she'd brought nothing but trouble to him and Langden's. "We have a company to run and, because of me, that company and Cade have been targeted, too."

"You don't need to worry about me or the company. You know we have our own trustworthy security team, and we'll weather this threat just like any other," said Cade.

"Without me?" she tossed back at him, stiffening. She started to withdraw from his embrace. "Is that what you're suggesting? That we'd both be safer if I didn't come back to Dallas with you? You think I should just hide?"

He frowned and started to speak, but Lynette interrupted. "Please. Let's not worry about it tonight. I'm guessing you two planned a long weekend, so please stay with us and enjoy the next couple days," she pleaded.

Sallie's eyes widened in amazement. "How am I supposed to relax and pretend nothing has happened?" She glanced from one to the other of her parents, her tone growing uncharacteristically harsh. "You had me watched for five years! You broke your promise, and you've basically financed a madman to stalk me and cause incalculable damage to Langden's. How am I supposed to handle that? Oops, sorry?"

"We did what was necessary," grumbled Carlton belligerently. "We had no way of knowing how treacherous Carmichael could be."

"That's just it, it wasn't necessary," Sallie argued heatedly. "I would have been perfectly safe without your interference. I'd been living a comfortable, *normal* life until your hired thug turned rogue!"

"Believe me, we are more sorry than you'll ever know." Lynette stepped in to referee between her strong-willed husband and equally strong-willed daughter. "Life is full of lessons and some of them are really hard ones," she said with a catch in her voice.

"Being a parent doesn't mean you always make the right choices," she continued after clearing her throat. "You make mistakes, sometimes with grave consequences, but you never stop learning and trying to do better. We owe you an apology for not being totally honest from the beginning, but if we had to do it over, I'm not sure we'd do anything differently. You are our whole world and we adore you. We'll do anything in our power to protect you."

A short silence fell after her mother's impassioned declaration. Sallie slumped against Cade with a sigh. As the anger slowly seeped out of her, his arms enfolded her more securely.

Then her dad leaned forward and spoke directly to Cade. Sallie tensed again, recognizing the man-to-man expression and his sudden change in demeanor. He'd quickly morphed into what her mother called his business mode.

"Since Carmichael is still in my employ, I'll take full responsibility for his acts of vandalism at Langden's and make financial restitution for damages you incurred at his hands."

"I appreciate the offer, but our insurance should cover

most the costs. I'm not even sure what that will be yet," Cade told him.

Carlton nodded, and then grew more serious. "I've been following the growth and success of your company," he declared.

Lynette groaned and tried to hush him. He absently patted her hand and continued. "I'm not easily impressed, but I know you started with little more than an engineering design and have worked diligently to create a thriving business. I admire the kind of hard work and determination it takes to succeed in today's economy."

Such an admission from a corporate icon like her father was high praise. Sallie glanced up at Cade and noticed the tint of a blush on his cheeks. She couldn't remember ever seeing him blush. Apparently her father's admiration meant a great deal to him. That both surprised and worried her.

"I've had a lot of great advice and employee support," said Cade. "Sallie's help has been invaluable, so I'm sure I owe part of that success to you and Mrs. Harriman."

Sallie smiled slightly at the way her dad nodded, accepting the fact that genetics played an important role in her business acumen. She'd always wished she'd been endowed with some wonderful creative talent rather than a head for business.

"Sallie's probably mentioned that I've always wanted her to take the reins at Harriman's, but she refuses to work with me."

Cade stiffened a little, and Sallie cringed. Her dad had

hit on a sore subject since she'd kept her true identity from him so long. She eased from his arms and braced herself for her dad's next words.

"This may not be the best time, but I'd like to extend an open invitation for you to join my organization," said Carlton. "I need dependable, trustworthy people at the helm now that I'm semi-retired. I'd be happy to incorporate Langden's into the Harriman fold. I'm willing to pay a price that will make you independently wealthy and throw in a handsome annual salary, as well. You and Sallie make a great team. I think you'd thrive on the opportunity for professional growth."

Sallie wanted to protest. She wanted to scream in frustration and shout out the unfairness of the offer, to accuse her father of blatant bribery. He was a master manipulator, and he'd always wanted her under his control. Now he'd changed tactics and wanted to control her through Cade. She loved him dearly, but at that very minute, she badly wanted to give him another piece of her mind.

Instead, she bit her lip, hard, hoping Cade would reject the offer. He had to know that she didn't want any part of the deal. She wanted him to resist temptation, but he'd just told her that his greatest desire was to secure financially his Langden heritage. Her father had just handed him the means. If he accepted the buyout, he could secure the future of several generations of Langdens, with or without her approval.

But it wasn't his finances that interested her the most. Her heart sank when he told her father he'd give the proposition some serious thought. After that, she let the conversation flow around her without contributing much.

Sallie knew it was unfair to feel disappointed in Cade's reaction. Could she really blame him for not refusing the offer outright? On one hand, she'd love to have his unconditional support in the effort to keep a distance between herself and the Harriman fortune. On the other hand, he'd be a fool to take the offer lightly. From a business viewpoint, it was a once-in-a-lifetime opportunity.

Cade deserved the best, yet she hoped he cared enough about her to refuse. Maybe he just wanted to discuss the offer with her first. Or maybe he hadn't wanted to offend her dad with an outright refusal.

And why was she allowing it to bother her so much? She didn't intend to be part of some package deal between the two men. There were other jobs with other companies. She could leave Langden's and start fresh somewhere else if Cade decided to sell out to her dad.

In the back of her mind, she'd been considering the idea, anyway, knowing she couldn't continue to work with him once their relationship ended. Although the thought of it made her feel slightly ill, she didn't want to dwell on it too much. She'd decided to enjoy the ride as long as they were together and let the future take care of itself, even though the idea was totally foreign to her nature.

Right now, all the worrying and wondering just made her head hurt and her brain tired. The unaccustomed amount of brandy soon caught up with her, and she had to stifle a yawn.

"Are we boring you?" Cade asked, turning his attention back to her.

"To tell the truth, I haven't been paying much attention," she admitted, offering him a small smile. "I'm feeling a little tipsy, and I think I'm about ready to head for bed."

Carlton glanced at his watch and disagreed. "It's still early."

"It is not," chimed in Lynette. "And the kids have had a long day."

Kids? Sallie blinked and stared at her mother. Were her parents locked in some sort of time-warp or was she just overly sensitive? A little of both, maybe?

"You'll have plenty of time to visit tomorrow and it wouldn't hurt you to have an early night, either," Lynette told her husband as she rose to her feet.

Cade rose and offered Sallie a hand. She let him draw her to her feet and then she swayed a little, earning herself a big grin from him. "I think you are a little tipsy," he said.

"All the more reason to take me to bed," she told him, returning his smile with one of feigned innocence.

Cade chuckled, and Sallie thought he might be blushing again. She momentarily left his side to give both her parents a peck on the cheek. They all said their goodnights, and she latched onto his arm again as they left the room. They were quiet as they headed down the hallway. When they reached her bedroom door, Sallie turned her back to it and faced Cade.

"Sorry if I embarrassed you, but it's time my parents started seeing me as an adult rather than their only child."

He put his arms around her waist and drew her body close to him. "Don't tell me I'm being used as a form of daughterly rebellion," he said, brushing a kiss across her lips.

Sallie swayed closer and locked her arms around his neck. She pressed her abdomen against his and was pleased to feel the instant hardening of his body in response to her closeness. It brought a sultry smile to her features as she looked up at him.

"Been there, done that, and I'm not interested in repeating the mistake," she murmured, nibbling on his lips.

Cade slid his hands to her hips and drew her closer. "So what does that make me?"

"It makes you a very desirable man," she said. "Not an overeager schoolboy."

"Mmm...I like the sound of that," he said against her lips. "But I thought you were tired and a little drunk. I don't want to be accused of taking advantage of a lady while she's under the influence."

"Mmm...The only influence I'm under right now is the spell of a very hot, sexy guy."

"A very needy guy." He pinned her against the door with his lower body, freeing his hands to fondle her breasts. He cupped them through the silky fabric of her gown and molded them with his palms until she purred like a kitten.

Her nipples stiffened, straining against the fabric for more of his touch. Sallie locked her hands on either side of his face and dragged his mouth to hers for a long, searing kiss that had them both panting for breath.

"Damn, woman, you go to my head faster than anyone I've ever known," he whispered gruffly. "The hours since we were naked together have seemed like an eternity. Do you think we could make love again real soon so I can sink myself into your sweet, welcoming heat?"

His words and the obvious hunger behind them sent an arrow of heat deep inside of her. She loved having him at her mercy, if only temporarily. The feminine sexual power was heady stuff.

Sallie laughed lightly and reached behind her for the handle of her door. She thought, briefly, about refusing him, but then laughed at the ridiculousness of the thought. Refusing him would be denying herself pleasure beyond description, and she didn't feel like self-denial. She wanted him as badly.

Opening the door, she moved inside and drew him in with her. He quickly reversed their positions and pressed her against the door again, locking her in place with forceful pressure. He didn't try to mask the strength of his erection, but ground it between her thighs until they were moaning into each other's mouths.

The room was dark except for a glimmer of moonlight, so they made love with a form of Braille, using their hands to guide them over familiar territory. Cade continued to kiss her, using his tongue to probe every inch of her mouth. He slid the shoulders of her gown down her arms, and then gasped for breath.

"I've been dying all night, knowing you weren't wearing a bra under this beautiful dress."

"I'm not wearing much at all under this dress," she whispered, lashing his lips with her tongue. She smiled when he moaned.

Cade pulled her close to his chest and reached behind her to slowly pull down the zipper. Once loosened, the gown started slipping off her shoulders, baring her breasts. He cupped them, molded them with his palms and then dipped his head to lash each nipple with his hot tongue.

"I always thought women exaggerated when they said their knees went weak," she whispered, clutching Cade's hair in her fists, needing an anchor of support.

He dipped his tongue into the valley of her breasts, and then laved a damp path up her throat to her mouth. "I hope I've destroyed that misconception," he murmured roughly before stealing another long, leisurely kiss.

"Uh-huh..." she said when they finally broke for air. "I want you naked." Now her hands were impatient, tugging his shirt over his chest and off his arms.

"You first," he insisted, stepping back far enough to let her gown fall the rest of the way off her body.

Their eyes had adjusted to the darkness enough to allow him a better look at her. She wore only the tiniest of thong panties. He groaned, and then moved closer again. Grasping her buttocks, he massaged them until he drew moans from deep in her throat.

They both shed their shoes as he carried her to the bed. Cade fell backward onto the mattress and pulled her along his body. The naked-chest-to-naked-chest contact had them uttering moans of pleasure into each other's mouths as they sank into another kiss. It was long and deep and each of them strained for more closeness.

Sallie twined her legs with his, savoring the roughness of his pants against her bare flesh. She rubbed herself against the strength of his arousal until she heard as well as felt a deep rumble from his chest. Then she slipped her hands between them to unfasten his slacks. Cade quickly turned them both on their sides until he could shuck his pants and briefs. He just as quickly pulled her back along his naked body. His hands went to her hips to rid her of her panties.

"You make me weak, too," he swore gruffly. "It works both ways. You make me so hungry for the feel of you that I never get enough. I always want more. I want to bury myself in you and stay as close as I can get."

Sallie stilled and stared into his eyes. She saw the truth in his features and the strain of sexual hunger. She didn't doubt his words because she felt the same way. He'd become a fever in her blood. It was awesome and it scared her to hell.

"How long, Cade?" she asked hoarsely. "You have more experience than I do. How long does this insatiable hunger last? How long before the lust turns lukewarm? How long before the sexual tension fizzles and we start to lose interest?"

He didn't answer in words, but captured her mouth in a long, hard kiss while he slid his hand between her legs. He sucked her tongue into his mouth and caressed her with sure strokes until she writhed against him in impatience. When she cried out his name, he thrust into her with a strength and sureness that made her forget everything but hot sensation and soaring pleasure.

When they were both sated and panting for breath, he drew her into his arms and held her tightly. Pressing his mouth to her ear, he answered her earlier question. "I don't know how long," he said on rasping breaths. "I lost all objectivity the first time you came apart in my arms. I don't know how long it will take to tamp the fires you light in me, but I think it could be a very, very long time."

Sallie nodded, snuggling closer. She believed him because she felt the same way. She trusted him because he didn't offer her empty promises. Neither of them could predict the future.

Chapter Eleven

Late Sunday afternoon, Sallie and Cade returned to Dallas. As soon as they'd received word that Carmichael had been apprehended, they headed to the airport. Her parents wanted her to stay in Phoenix a while longer, but she badly needed some time alone with Cade.

He'd been unusually reserved since their in-depth discussion with her parents. The business proposal, along with more insight into her background, had definitely taken him by surprise. She wanted to know what he was thinking and feeling, but he didn't offer any clues.

Did he think her a freak? Did her family's filthy rich lifestyle appall him? Had he glimpsed the world of the rich and famous and hated it? Or worse, did he aspire to it himself? The kind of power her dad wielded could be alluring. Hadn't she learned that lesson the hard way?

How could she convince him that it wasn't her world when it was obvious she couldn't completely remove herself from their world? He'd been a polite, considerate guest while they were in her parents' house, but she wanted the intimacy they'd shared on the ranch.

When they reached Sallie's house, they were greeted

by two young police officers. Cade identified himself and exchanged brief introductions.

"We heard that the stalker's been arrested. Anything suspicious happening around here?"

"We were assigned to keep an eye on the place, but it's been really quiet," explained one officer. "I did a perimeter check a couple of minutes ago and didn't see any sign of trouble."

The second officer added, "We just got a call about the apprehension, too, and we got orders to return to our regular beat."

Before he'd completed the sentence, his radio crackled with a message that Sallie couldn't decipher. The first officer turned to the second. "Armed robbery at the jewelers in Metro Mall."

With a nod and quick farewell, they raced toward the cruiser parked on the street.

Cade and Sallie watched them leave and then slowly approached her front door. "Give me your keys. I'll go in first and do a quick check of the house," he said.

The unprecedented tension between them had them both on edge. It seemed days since they'd enjoyed a private conversation. Flying always exhausted Sallie and this time it had given her a headache that compounded her stress level. She handed over her keys without an argument.

Cade stepped inside the door, flipped on the lights and set down her suitcases. She followed him across the threshold, but turned her back to him while she keyed in the new security code. Then she heard the unmistakable sound of something solid making contact with a human skull. She whirled as his grunt of pain was followed by the thud of his body falling to the floor.

"Cade!" she screamed in panic as the door slammed and a big, beefy hand grabbed her arm to stop her from going to his prone body. "Let go of me!" She tried to wrench herself free, but quickly stilled when she found herself facing the barrel of a very big gun.

"You're not giving the orders today, little missy."

Sallie's heart lurched when she realized she'd come face-to-face with Carmichael. He stared at her with eyes that sat too close together on his face. He had dark, bushy brows, a tight mouth and several days' growth of beard. He smelled of cigarette smoke and sweat. His fingers gripped her with bruising strength.

"You've hurt Cade," she accused shrilly. "Let go of me!"

This time he allowed her to jerk from his grip, and she dropped to the floor beside Cade. He had a nasty gash at the back of his head that was oozing blood. Her stomach roiled at the thought that he might be badly injured and it was her fault. She silently whispered an apology, but vowed not to say anything more to the madman who had done this to him. How could Carmichael be free already? Hadn't the police assured them that everything was under control? How had he gotten past the officers posted outside her house? What had gone wrong?

Just then, Carmichael slammed a kitchen chair

beside Cade's body, making her flinch and realize that she had to do something to get them out of this mess. She had to think hard and not let her fear for Cade blur her senses. She couldn't panic and she couldn't be immobilized by fear. *I won't be immobilized by fear!* She mentally chanted the old refrain.

"I want him tied to the chair," said Carmichael.

She looked up at him in amazement. "He's unconscious. I can't lift him."

"Take one arm and I'll take the other. I didn't hit him that hard. He's coming to already, so he can help himself to his feet."

Sallie glanced back at Cade. He was starting to stir and that scared her even more. What would this maniac do to him next? She reached for his left arm to help him steady himself and Carmichael grabbed his right arm to haul him toward the straight-back chair. Then Carmichael all but shoved him onto the seat.

"Cade, be careful. He's got a gun." Sallie stroked his arm, trying to soothe him and warn him at the same time.

"Quit fussing over him and tape him up." He handed her a roll of gray duct tape. "Tape his ankles to the legs of the chair and then his hands behind his back. Don't try anything stupid, or I'll put a bullet in him."

Sallie's hands trembled as she did as she was told, tightly wrapping the thick tape around Cade's booted feet and then to the legs of the chair. She knew Carmichael was willing to murder in cold blood. Hadn't he already done it several times? Her whole body shook with fear for the man she loved and fury at the man who'd invaded her life and home. She silently vowed to make him pay.

Waving the gun, Carmichael motioned her to tape his hands next. "Behind your back," he growled at Cade, who had regained enough consciousness to reach a hand to the wound on his head. When Cade's expression grew angry and belligerent, Carmichael repositioned the gun until it was pointed at Sallie's head. Cade slowly did as he was told, never losing eye contact with Carmichael.

Sallie was relieved to see the clarity returning to Cade's eyes and happy that the two men tried to stare each other down while she taped Cade's wrists. She wrapped them in a single smooth pattern, but then used the edge of her fingernail to make a notch at the bottom of the tape. She knew that once the outer edge of duct tape was slit, the rest would rip apart if enough pressure could be applied. It was the only thing she could think to do at the moment.

"Now get away from him!" Carmichael returned his attention to her.

Sallie rose to her feet and moved around the chair again. She flashed a glance at Cade. His expression urged her to cooperate and not take any chances. They both knew help would arrive soon. They had too many people prepared to intervene if they weren't heard from within minutes of arriving at her house. Besides, if Carmichael had escaped from custody, the Dallas police would be looking for him, too.

She knew they needed to be calm, to find out what

Carmichael had planned and to avoid any further bloodshed. Her stomach still hadn't stopped churning from seeing the man she loved being knocked unconscious and bleeding.

The man she loved. Sallie stared at him in surprise and awe. She loved Cade. Not just as a lover, but as a man she couldn't bear to live without. A man for whom she'd be willing to do anything to keep safe. The realization and the crazy timing of it had her stunned to silence for an instant.

Cade frowned at her, and she knew he thought she was losing it. In a way, she was. She glanced at Carmichael and realized that she didn't consider him as much a threat to her as the shocking knowledge she'd just discovered about herself. She was deeply, hopelessly in love with a man who probably wouldn't appreciate the sentiment. Hysteria threatened and she forced herself to concentrate on their precarious situation.

"I thought the police had you locked up," said Cade.

"Idiots," scoffed Carmichael, his gaze swinging back and forth between them. He didn't look the least bit nervous, just frighteningly cold and calculating. "All I did was a little identity exchange with a wino with burned fingers and a messed-up face. There's no way to do a positive ID until he heals in a couple of days. By that time, I'll be long gone."

"How'd you get past the officers posted outside?"

"Weekend warriors," he snarled. "Stupid rookies sat out front most of the time. They didn't see me come in and nobody's gonna see me leave."

"Where are you planning to go?"

The barrel-chested man laughed and turned the gun back on Cade. Sallie's heart missed a beat, and then another, her pulse rioting in her temples and through her body.

"I'm not planning to tell you anything, Langden. You've become a real pain in my ass. You'll just have to sit there and burn when Sallie and I leave. Her house is about to go up in flames."

Sallie glared at Carmichael, but she wouldn't give him the satisfaction of asking a question or showing any interest in him at all. If he craved her attention, that's the last thing she planned on giving him.

"She doesn't have anything to say to you. Or haven't you figured that out yet?" Cade taunted.

Sallie knew he was trying to stall for time. Alec was at the police department attempting to identify the man who'd been arrested. They'd called Steven when they left the airport. Either or both of them would be here soon.

Carmichael ignored his comment. "Cat got your tongue, little princess?"

She quickly turned her head so he couldn't see her face, but sent Cade a quick, questioning glance. Did the madman's mention of a cat remind him of Jasper as it had to her? Her cat would be nearby and watching. She turned slightly and noticed Jasper's favorite stuffed snake on the floor. It was just a foot or two behind Carmichael. If she could get him to step on it, Jasper would undoubtedly pounce. It might be enough of a distraction to throw Carmichael off balance so that she could knock the weapon from his hand.

"Giving me the silent treatment?" Carmichael's tone changed, deepening into the low, intimate tone he'd used to harass her on the telephone. It sent a shudder through Sallie, but she managed a disdainful expression for him.

Her attitude infuriated him. His gun remained steadily pointed at Cade's head, but malevolence glittered in his eyes when he looked at her. "One of these days, soon, you're going to realize how much you need me, little princess. You've always needed me. Not your daddy or your boss here or any other man. Just me."

"What I need is for you to get out of my house."

Carmichael laughed roughly, his gaze momentarily shifting to encompass the room. "Not going to happen. Nice place you have here. Too bad it has to be destroyed."

Sallie took the opportunity to make eye contact with Cade. He gave her the briefest of nods, and she knew he'd understood her silent communication. She hoped he'd managed to get his hands free. His feet were still bound to the chair, but if Jas could pounce and distract Carmichael, Cade could launch himself forward. They might be able to throw him off balance enough to overpower him. If not, help would be arriving soon, but that would have them tangled in an even nastier hostage situation.

"Come here," ordered Carmichael, motioning for her to step further from Cade and closer to him.

"Put down the gun," she countered.

"Maybe you should come a little closer and ask me real nice," he said when he noticed her edging further from him. He briefly turned his attention from Cade and took a step backward to keep her in his view. She backed further away. He took another step, and his foot landed squarely on Jas's squeaky snake.

Then all hell broke loose. Jas flew from under the couch in full attack mode, squalling and lashing Carmichael's leg with razor-sharp claws. At the same time, Cade launched himself forward, managing to ram his head into Carmichael's midsection, knocking him to the floor. Sallie swiftly stomped on the hand holding his gun and it went flying across the floor.

Sirens could be heard in the distance and she was vaguely aware of help approaching as she scrambled to get the gun. Cade and Carmichael wrestled viciously until she screamed for Cade to back off. He twisted sideways, trying to break the hold Carmichael had on him. At the same time, Sallie aimed Carmichael's own gun at his head and started shouting.

"Don't even think about moving anymore," she screamed harshly. "I will put a bullet in your ugly, evil brain."

Carmichael relaxed his grip on Cade and stared at her. "You don't have the guts," he challenged, but he didn't move a muscle.

"I'm battling more with my conscience than courage or fear," she told him darkly. "I know I shouldn't shoot you now that you've been disarmed, but I really, really want you dead."

Carmichael looked taken aback by her vehemence. He didn't so much as blink an eye as she continued.

"You murdered my brother." Her voice trembled with rage. She had no evidence, yet instinct had her challenging him to learn the depth of his involvement. "Kidnapped and murdered a defenseless child you were supposed to be protecting. And then you continued to ingratiate yourself with me and my parents. You're the scum of the earth and you deserve to die. You've taken my father's money and harassed me for months. You're too evil and loathsome to live, but a quick bullet to the brain is way too good for you. Maybe I'll start on your kneecaps. Isn't that how you taught me to cause the most pain?"

Carmichael's eyes began to glitter. "So you do remember me," he said with satisfaction. "You were a bothersome teenager, but you grew into a very desirable woman. As your protector, I deserved to marry into those millions. You'll see. We're meant to be together. I've been planning it for years."

"Just like you planned Brent's kidnapping and murder?"

"I didn't kill Brent! It was an accident!" Carmichael protested.

"But you don't deny kidnapping him?"

"I just planned to keep him a little while and then rescue him!"

"What? So you could collect the ransom and then play

the hero?"

The thought made Sallie go a little crazy. Something inside of her snapped and the scene took on a surreal quality. The blood roared in her ears with the violent pounding of her pulse. She was vaguely aware of Cade struggling to free himself from the chair, but her attention was riveted on her murderous intruder.

"You're insane!" she yelled. "I promised Brent's cold, lifeless body that if I ever got the chance, I'd make his kidnapper pay." With that, she fired the gun. Carmichael yowled in pain and clutched his kneecap. Sallie shuddered at the gun's recoil, but then regained her balance and aimed at his other leg.

The gun shook as she trembled in anger, but she quickly steadied it.

Carmichael's voice quivered as he clung to his injured leg and defended his actions. "Brent would have been fine if he hadn't tried to escape. His death was an accident, I tell you!"

"Now you're blaming my brother for his own death?" Her voice went raw and hoarse, his excuses making her more furious. She fired again, but her vision was so blurred by tears that her shot went astray. The bullet struck the floor next to his good leg, but she drew satisfaction from Carmichael's scream of fear.

"Sallie, give me the gun."

Cade had freed himself from the chair and moved to her side. His low tone pierced the haze of her anger. She heard shouting and hammering on the door, realizing that the sound of the gunshots would have her rescuers feeling desperate.

"You need to hand the gun to me and open the door for the police before they break it down."

Cade's calm, reasonable voice finally got through her blinding haze of fury. A thud at the door caught her attention next. The police were trying to break it down. She shot a blistering glance at Carmichael and carefully passed the gun to Cade. "If he moves, shoot him again," she instructed with grim determination.

"Stop ramming my door!" she yelled fiercely, knowing it wouldn't be easy for them to break down the steel-reinforced door. Nor would it be cheap to replace.

"We're okay," she yelled. "Everything's okay! I'm coming!"

A small army of police officers along with her dad's security team was on her doorstep and swarming her yard. Lights blazed in blinding brilliance. She blinked, trying to reorient herself after being lost in a fit of fury unlike anything she'd ever experienced. Several officers entered the house while others motioned to paramedics. Carmichael was quickly handcuffed and read his rights.

The medics asked if she was okay, but she shrugged off their concern. She nodded to Cade. "He has a gash on the back of his head that needs attention." She didn't give a thought to the injury she'd done Carmichael except to wish she'd shot his other leg while she had the chance.

"Sallie! Sallie!" he still begged for her attention, but she deliberately ignored him, determined to squash any fantasy he'd ever had about them belonging together.

Cade handed the gun over to the officer in charge and started answering questions while a paramedic cleaned and dressed his wound. He evaded questions about who shot Carmichael. She knew he wanted to protect her, but she didn't want him to take the blame for something she'd done.

She'd straighten it out later, but her legs were threatening to fold under her right now. Sitting down in her favorite chair, she called softly to Jas. It took a little time, but he finally crept from his hiding place and jumped into her lap. She crooned softly to him, telling him what a brave guard cat he'd been and how he'd saved the day. She slowly, methodically stroked his fur and kept murmuring silly, mindless things.

Alec Walker and Steven Tanner finally shoved past the police barricades and made their way into the house. Cade talked to them, too, but his gaze kept darting back to her. He watched her with a grim, worried expression.

Sallie wanted to reassure him, to tell him not to worry. She'd be okay. She'd shocked them both with her deliberate act of brutality, but she wasn't sorry. She felt absolutely no guilt. If she hadn't had a gun to use on Brent's murderer, she'd have scratched his eyes out or tried to beat him with her bare hands.

She hoped Cade wouldn't think less of her or that she was some kind of crazed vigilante. Carmichael had robbed her family of so much. He'd taken her brother's life. So much pain and heartache. He deserved every horrible thing life could throw at him. His body should rot in prison and then his soul, if he had one, should rot in hell.

༄༅༄༅

Hours later, Cade opened the door to his apartment and ushered Sallie into his home. He dropped their cases and hit the light switch, illuminating a big living room with very traditional furnishings. The combination of browns, blues and beige offered a warm, earthy welcome after the chaos they'd just suffered.

The ride from her home to his had been made in relative silence. They were beyond exhausted.

"I'm really sorry I insisted on stopping at my place for fresh clothes," she told him without looking at him.

"I'm sorry you had to deal with Carmichael, but I'm not sorry we have that behind us now," Cade said on a sigh.

Sallie turned to face him. "You're the one who had to deal with the worst of him," she argued apologetically. "I wish you would have gone to the hospital."

"I'm fine," he assured her. "I told you my head's too hard to suffer much damage."

"Cade," she scolded him for making light of his injury.

He took one look at the concern etched on her features and changed tactics. "I promise I'm fine. If I had a concussion, I'd have a whopper of a headache. All I feel is a little tenderness."

She continued to stare into his eyes. After another minute, she relaxed a little and nodded. There was so much more she wanted to say, but she didn't trust her voice right now.

Cade seemed to sense her fragile composure. He gave her a smile and turned her toward a door to the left of the living room. "My room and the master bath are this way," he said as he drew her along with him. "I have a giant tub with lots of massaging jets."

"One of those really decadent sauna-type bathtubs?"

"You bet," he teased as he switched on the bedroom light. "Why don't you go fill it to the brim and relax a while?"

"Sounds wonderful."

Sallie gave his bedroom a cursory glance, noting the tasteful navy and maroon décor. It had a very masculine, sparsely furnished look that suited Cade perfectly.

He moved ahead of her to turn on the light in the bathroom and set her overnight case inside the door. "Help yourself to anything you need."

The thought of him leaving her, even briefly, caused a totally unexpected flare of panic. She grasped his arm. "You're not joining me?"

Their gazes connected for a long minute. Sallie wasn't sure what he saw in her eyes, but he reached out to stroke her face with his thumb. "I thought you might like some privacy," he whispered gruffly.

She didn't say anything, but maintained eye contact and slowly shook her head from side-to-side.

As she watched, some of the tension seemed to drain from Cade's face and body. He gave her a warm, deep smile.

"Why don't you fill up the tub while I get us something to drink? I'll be right back."

"Promise?"

"You bet."

Sallie returned his smile, but hers was still a little shaky. Cade dipped his head and brushed a reassuring kiss across her lips. "I'll be back before you can miss me," he swore.

She watched him leave and wondered if he realized how wrong he was about that. Or how shocked he'd be if he knew the truth. That she was totally, unbelievable crazy about him and that she missed him before he was even out of sight.

Did that make her a complete fool? Just one of the many women who adored him? Another woman who wanted anything he was willing to offer? What if tonight's fiasco had convinced him to steer clear of her in the future? She wished she could read his emotions better. They'd always had such a great professional rapport, but she couldn't judge his private thoughts or concerns.

Sighing, she turned to the tub and started the water. After adjusting the jets, she stripped. Too bone weary to care about her clothes, she shed them in a puddle on the floor and stepped into the tub. A moan of pleasure escaped her as she eased herself neck-deep into the hot, churning water.

Her eyes had just started to close when Cade reentered the room. He handed her a glass of red wine.

"Comfy?" he asked.

She nodded her head and took a sip of wine. "Coming in?" she asked.

His eyes darkened at the invitation. "Are you sure you're up to it? I don't think I'll be able to share your bath and not want your body," he warned.

"I'm tired, but not dead," she murmured softly.

In response, Cade treated her to a very slow, extremely arousing strip show. Sallie watched the layers of clothes drop to the floor and enjoyed every inch of masculine flesh being revealed. She wanted all of it pressed close to her and she got her wish within minutes. As soon as the final article of clothing hit the floor, he stepped into the tub and slid down behind her. His arms came around her as his legs slid to either side of her hips. She leaned back against his chest.

"Mmm...that's really nice," she said as she drained her wine glass. Warmth seeped inside her as well as outside, and she dropped her head to his shoulder.

Cade mumbled in agreement. The swirling water quickly worked its magic on their bodies, and Sallie felt his muscles going lax. For a few minutes, they were satisfied to enjoy the sensual pleasure and closeness. Then he broached the subject of the evening's events.

"Alec said your parents won't be satisfied until they see you and assure themselves you're all right."

That didn't surprise her. She'd phoned them earlier,

but she'd refused to fly back to Phoenix with Alec. "They'll have to come here because I'm home, and I'm staying home."

Cade locked his arms over her chest and tightened his hold on her. His tone went low as he spoke near her ear. "You think of Dallas as your home?"

"Of course," she murmured drowsily. "Don't you?"

"Not really," he explained. "The ranch will always be home for me. Dallas is where I live and work most of the time. I thought maybe you felt the same about your family home."

"My family had several properties for all the seasons of the year," she said. "I considered the New York estate my home when Brent and I were younger. After he died, it became a gilded cage."

"I can't imagine what it must have been like for you to lose your brother."

Sallie fought back the sudden rush of tears and swallowed hard.

"I thought I was over the worst of the grief years ago," she said. "But tonight..." She paused to swallow more tears. "Tonight, all the pain came rushing back with a vengeance. All the agonizing days of waiting for word of Brent. The media circus, the horror when his body was found, and then the long, terrible funeral week. It was a nightmare."

Once she started talking, she couldn't stop the outpouring of emotion. "I thought I'd matured and put all that behind me. I saw a therapist for a few months after his death, and I understood about survivor's guilt. I had no idea I was still harboring so much pent-up rage. Tonight, when Carmichael hurt you, all that impotent fury seemed to bombard me at once. I know you think I'm a total lunatic because I shot him and I'm not even sorry. I wanted to hurt him. I wanted him to suffer. Is that horrible? Does that make me as evil a person as he is?"

A sob escaped her and Cade turned her until she could face him. "Shh... You're not evil," he assured her, then brushed damp hair from her face. He wiped away a tear that trickled down her cheek. "You're a perfectly normal, healthy adult who had to deal with more emotion than anyone should have to handle. I don't blame you one bit for shooting that maniac."

"Really? You didn't think I'd lost my mind?"

"I wouldn't have cared if you put a hole in his head," Cade declared flatly. "I just didn't want you to have to deal with the consequences. I think you showed considerable restraint."

Sallie gave him a slow smile. "He's lucky I missed with the second shot."

He smiled back at her. "You were incredibly brave, and you saved us both from what could have been a long, nasty hostage situation."

"I wasn't brave, I was furious, and I wasn't going to let him hurt you. He's already hurt all the people I love the most in the world."

Cade went very still. He searched her face intently. When he spoke, his voice was raw with emotion. "You don't know how much I want to be among the people you love the most."

Sallie's response was breathless. "Really?"

"Really. I'm so desperate for your love that I'm ready to promise you anything, do anything that will make you want me half as much as I want you." He drew in a deep breath and then added, "Marry me?"

They stared into each other's eyes for a long, silent minute, each stilled and watchful. Water churned around and over them, yet they seemed frozen in stillness. Sallie searched his features for some inkling of the emotion behind the proposal, but his expression didn't give her a clue to what he was feeling. He'd said he wanted her to love him and asked her to marry him, but he hadn't mentioned loving her in return.

Her mind flashed back five years to a desolate motel in upstate New York. Derrick had persuaded her to elude her bodyguard and run away with him. She'd trusted him enough to agree, but she'd gotten cold feet when it came to actually having sex. Instead of calming her fears, he'd forced himself on her physically. He'd decided he was going to coerce her into marriage or a pregnancy.

For years, she'd blamed herself for the loss of her innocence. Now she knew that she deserved so much more. Derrick had wanted to marry her, but he'd never really loved her. He'd been far more interested in becoming a wealthy, powerful member of the Harriman family. She'd just been a means to an end. He hadn't respected her at all.

The memory had Sallie slowly extricating herself from Cade's embrace and climbing from the tub. Her heart felt heavy in her chest. She wanted to be elated by the proposal. She wanted to believe in Cade, believe that he'd realized he loved her as much as she loved him. She wanted it more than her next breath, but she'd be the worst kind of fool if she made the same mistake again. She had to be certain.

Keeping her back to the tub, she wrapped herself in a big bath towel and forced the words past a tight throat. "Does your unexpected proposal have anything to do with my dad's offer of a position at Harriman's?"

Cade didn't immediately reply. Sallie stood rigid and waited while steam swirled around her and tears pooled in her eyes. Torn between the need for his love and the need for honesty, she wasn't sure how she wanted him to respond. She heard him shut off the jets and flip the drain lever. As he stepped out of the tub, he reached around her for another towel. Only then did she realize he was quietly furious.

His face, when she finally risked a glance at it, was frozen in anger; his jaw tight, his lips thinned. The emotion she'd wanted to see earlier now swirled in the dark depths of his eyes, but it wasn't the sort of emotional response she'd anticipated.

"That's what you really think of me?" he finally asked, his voice tight with angry tension. "After five years of working side-by-side in countless situations, you've decided that I'm a man with no moral fiber? You consider me a lowlife who's willing to prey on a woman's emotions just to line my pockets? How the hell can you judge me that harshly? What have I ever done to make you think I'm so mercenary?"

His questions were punctuated with brisk swipes of a towel over his limbs and torso. Sallie watched in numb fascination as he quickly dried the excess water from his body, turned his back on her and stormed from the bathroom. She heard him slamming drawers in the bedroom, but she didn't make a move.

Clutching the towel with a hand fisted above her breasts, she swiped the tears from her face, trembling from head-to-toe. She bit her lip while considering his questions, and knew he was right. It was totally unfair of her to compare him to Derrick, who'd been little more than a spoiled schoolboy driven by ambition.

In her mind, she knew Cade to be one of the finest men she'd ever met. He was decent and honest and caring, yet the history of his relationships daunted her. He had so much more experience than she did. Why would he want her for a wife? Marriage meant forever and forever was a very, very long time.

The fear of pain and rejection still lingered in her heart. Her own insecurities were at the root of the problem, and Cade certainly couldn't be blamed for those. Since becoming lovers, he'd made her feel so feminine, sexy and desirable. She really needed to apologize.

Before she could formulate an apology, he came back into the bathroom and confronted her again. He'd pulled on clean shorts and a white T-shirt. His hair looked finger-combed from frustration. He looked clean, tousled, furious and gorgeous.

"You think I can be bought?" he snapped, stepping directly in front of her. He reached out and cupped her head gently, but firmly between his hands. Tension radiated from every inch of his big body.

"Do you think I proposed marriage to every wealthy woman I've ever known? Just hoping someone would offer me financial security? Do you think you're the only woman whose father ever tried to buy me for his daughter?"

The question took her by surprise, widening her eyes and mouth. She'd been so wrapped up in her own poor little rich girl scenario that she hadn't thought too much about his past lovers. "Someone else tried to buy you?" she squeaked out the question. "What did you tell them?"

His jaw clenched a little tighter. "That I wasn't for sale."

His response sent a tremor of pleasure over her, and she finally allowed herself to relax a little. She trusted Cade. Trusted him with her life and her heart. Now she needed to find a way to undo the harm she'd done with her initial panic at the mention of marriage. Not an easy thing to do considering how vulnerable love could make a person feel.

"Why?" Her tone took on a low, coaxing tone. She wanted the words he'd neglected to give her along with the proposal. She desperately needed reassurance. "Financial independence and security are your ultimate goals in life, and a lot of people have married for lesser reasons. Why now? Why me?"

As suddenly as Cade's anger had erupted, it evaporated. The turbulence in his eyes took on a different quality. The warmth in the dark depths shimmered with understanding.

"Did I forget to mention that I'm head over heels in love with you?" he asked her as he stepped close enough for their bodies to brush.

His words brought a lump to her throat. She couldn't squeeze an answer past it, so she slowly nodded. Then she turned her head and pressed a kiss against his palm. The simple caress brought a moan of pleasure from him.

Sallie finally managed to speak to him in a tear-filled voice. "I didn't even realize how much I loved you until Carmichael hurt you tonight." She let go of the towel and slid an arm around his waist as a shudder ripped through her. Cade pulled her into his arms and tried to hush her, but she wanted to offer him some reassurance, too.

"I confess that I never imagined we'd both end up wanting a long-term commitment. It's going to take me a little time to readjust my thinking. You know how anal I am."

Cade gave her one of the beautiful, sexy smiles that she treasured.

"I knew you didn't have much faith in our relationship from the beginning, and I know you're wary about making commitments," he added gruffly. "I planned to give you more time. To give us more time. But then your father started bartering with me and that madman pointed a gun at you. I went possessive and ballistic. All I wanted to do was bring you home with me and lock out the rest of the world until I could make you want me the way I care for you."

"Oh, Cade!"

"I love you," he told her, brushing a kiss across her lips. "There's no time limit on the proposal. We can take it as slow or fast as you want—keep dating, move in together or start planning a wedding. I'm okay with letting you set the pace. I just want you by my side and in my bed."

"Exclusively?" she asked with a grin.

"Hell, yes!"

His quick, fierce retort made her giddy with delight. She still wondered about her ability to attract and keep a man like Cade, but she refused to allow doubts to cloud her happiness. Right here and right now, she felt loved and needed. He'd always made her feel incredibly unique and important, from the day he'd hired a total novice through the years of professional respect to the lover he'd become in the past few days. She didn't know what she'd done to deserve his love, but she intended to cherish and nurture it as long as she lived.

Cade captured her mouth with his, and Sallie wrapped her arms around his neck. The towel slowly slid down her body as he pulled her closer to his hard frame. The soft cotton of his T-shirt teased at her breasts, making her nipples harden against his chest. A shudder of desire coursed to the pit of her stomach as he cupped her buttocks and lifted her off her feet. Sallie deepened the kiss, thrusting her tongue into his mouth as he carried her into the bedroom and laid her across his bed.

"You're overdressed," she murmured huskily.

"Not for long." He was already tugging the shirt over his head and tossing it aside.

She reached for the waistband of his shorts and helped him shed those, too. Then they swallowed each other's sighs of satisfaction as the feminine softness of her skin slid against the masculine roughness of his. Legs tangled and hands roamed over familiar, yet eminently fascinating features. They kept the pace of their loving slow and gentle, with husky words of endearment and reaffirming tenderness.

Bodies melded as two became one.

"You never answered my question," Cade reminded her as he stilled until she could accept his deep, intimate invasion.

She found it difficult to focus on his words. He'd fired so many questions at her. "Which one?"

Cade stroked the damp tendrils of her hair from her face. He looked into her eyes and held her gaze. "Will you marry me?"

Sallie sensed an underlying vulnerability in his question that surprised and humbled her. She never wanted him to doubt her love. The feelings were awesome and unexplored, but she wanted to share every aspect of her newfound love with him. It would take a lifetime.

Tangling her fingers in his hair, she pulled his head down for a kiss that left them both breathless. She couldn't manage much more than a whispered syllable. "Yes."

He gave her a triumphant grin and caressed her with his mouth, his hands and his entire body. "Good."

Sallie agreed. So good. So very good. She held him tighter and arched herself against him with all her strength. Life didn't get much better than this.

About the Author

To learn more about the author of *Cade's Challenge* and its prequel, *On Wings of Love*, please visit www.BeckyBarker.com or send an email to write@beckybarker.com.

Look for these titles by
Becky Barker

Now Available

On Wings of Love

Can a psychic investigator disprove an accidental death before she and her lover are next to die?

A Killer's Agenda
© 2007 Anita M. Whiting

Brad Norton doesn't believe his aunt's death is the accidental shooting the police claim it to be. His instincts tell him there's a more sinister explanation. In order to get to the bottom of it, he's going to need professional help.

Pairing up with Alex Leahy, a clairvoyant private investigator, wasn't exactly in his plans. He didn't expect the fiery redhead to take over the case and get under his skin so quickly, but things happen fast when Alex is around.

Still, they can't plan a future together with a killer on the loose. When their investigation intensifies they bring him out of hiding. The danger grows to an entirely new level, however, when attempts are made on their lives.

With six deaths already confirmed, it's a race to stop their man before Alex and Brad are next on the list.

Available now in ebook and print from Samhain Publishing.

The sheriff has the hots for her prime suspect. What's a girl to do?

Too Good to be True
© *2007 Marie-Nicole Ryan*

Sheriff Rilla Devane has sworn to serve and protect, just as her father did before he was murdered. An influx of party drugs has killed two teenagers, but she has a suspect: handsome, rich newcomer Mackenzie Callahan, a published author seeking small-town atmosphere. To build her case, she moves closer to Mackenzie and his dangerous brand of seductive charm. She'll risk everything for her investigation, even when it means letting her guard down and falling for her suspect.

Mac Callahan lives and breathes for undercover work. But his last mission ended in near disaster, and he has one last chance to prove his value to the DEA. Taking sexy Sheriff Rilla to bed might ruin his career—or lead him to the love of his life.

Available now in ebook and print from Samhain Publishing.

Enjoy the following excerpt from To Good to be True...

"Let's impress this crowd with our terpsichorean prowess."

She scowled and muttered, "Just because you pretend you're a writer, you don't have to talk like one around me."

"Come on." He stood and held out his hand, palm up.

"You're almost as smooth as Rob Wyler." She smirked and placed her hand in his.

Mmm. Warm and strong.

"I'll show you smooth." He pulled her to his chest and took off in an easy one-two, one-two-three swaying glide around the small dance floor.

Her body was warm against his chest. "You're pretty good at this," he whispered in her ear.

"You're not so bad yourself." She gazed into his eyes. "I must say I'm surprised."

"Why? Haven't you found me skillful in other physical endeavors?"

"Have I complained?"

He laughed. "No, you haven't at that."

The music continued and he drew Rilla closer. Her body molded to his...and felt damned good. "Dare I say it? Your beeper hasn't gone off once tonight."

Her eyes widened. Placing an elegant finger to her lips, she shushed him. "You've done it now, but maybe not. This isn't a real date."

"It isn't?" Mac nuzzled her neck. "Hmm, sure feels like one."

She gave a small shake of her head. "No, it's a pretend date so we could backup Kit."

He turned to leave the dance floor "Well, that's it. Ready to leave?"

She laughed, a low sensual growl and tugged on his hand. "Oh, no, you don't. The music's still playing."

She slipped her arms around his waist and slid her hands into the back pockets of his jeans, cupped his ass and pressed against his dick.

"This is feeling less like pretend," he said. Pretend, hell—she was teasing him and having a great time. His dick was hard as a rock, and if she kept it up...

But damn, he loved this playful side of her. He couldn't help but wonder if they'd met under different circumstances...

Her head went back, revealing the long column of her neck. She laughed then emitted a delicious giggle which sent a searing jolt straight to his groin. Did she have any clue how she affected him? "You're having too much fun."

"Is that even possible?" Her eyes glittered with amusement.

Possible? He swung her around and headed for the door. "Let's find out."

The Porsche was parked along the side of the roadhouse in the shadows. They made it to the car.

Barely.

GET IT NOW

MyBookStoreAndMore.com
GREAT EBOOKS, GREAT DEALS... AND MORE!

Don't wait to run to the bookstore down the street, or waste time shopping online at one of the "big boys." Now, all your favorite Samhain authors are all in one place—at MyBookStoreAndMore.com. Stop by today and discover great deals on Samhain—and a whole lot more!

Samhain Publishing

WWW.SAMHAINPUBLISHING.COM

HOT STUFF

Discover Samhain!
THE HOTTEST NEW PUBLISHER ON THE PLANET

Romance, fantasy, mystery, thriller, mainstream and more—Samhain has more selection, hotter authors, and everything's available in both ebook and print.

Pick your favorite, sit back, and enjoy the ride!
Hot stuff indeed.

Samhain Publishing

WWW.SAMHAINPUBLISHING.COM

GREAT CHEAP FUN

Discover eBooks!
THE FASTEST WAY TO GET THE HOTTEST NAMES

Get your favorite authors on your favorite reader, long before they're out in print! Ebooks from Samhain go wherever you go, and work with whatever you carry—Palm, PDF, Mobi, and more.

SAMHAIN PUBLISHING LTD

WWW.SAMHAINPUBLISHING.COM